# The Priest's Well

Sara Alexi is the author of the Greek Village Series.
She divides her time between England and a small
village in Greece.

http://facebook.com/authorsaraalexi

Sara Alexi

# THE PRIEST'S WELL

## A Novella

oneiro

Published by Oneiro Press 2015

ISBN-13: **978-1514219799**

ISBN-10: **1514219794**

## Also by Sara Alexi

The Illegal Gardener
Black Butterflies
The Explosive Nature of Friendship
The Gypsy's Dream
The Art of Becoming Homeless
In the Shade of the Monkey Puzzle Tree
A Handful of Pebbles
The Unquiet Mind
Watching the Wind Blow
The Reluctant Baker
The English Lesson

The knife slices through with ease, the blue blade bright against the red. Nails just a little too long leave half-moon indentations on the skin's surface. The first cut releases liquid which trickles out over his fingers, making them glisten in the shaft of light that filters through the window. The flesh gives way as the knife slices through. Easing his fingertip grip, he puts down the knife to exchange it for a spoon with a serrated edge.

The spoon gouges deep, excavating, ripping the innards from the fleshy wall, rupturing the wholeness, devastating the beauty, releasing his tensions.

Why was the incident at the last post brought up? Was that necessary? Was it kind?

The innards spill out, caught in the bowl, until there is nothing but a limp, empty shell.

And here is the trick! Although this is an olive oil-based dish, he knows from experience that if he smears the inside of the tomato shell with butter now, at this point, it will add another subtle, rich layer to the flavour when it is cooked.

Savvas smears it liberally.

To be fair, the conversation was not really unkind. In fact, it was less negative than a lot of his superiors back in America. Some of those had been downright condemnatory.

The green parsley and the fresh, fuzzy-leafed mint release their aromas as he chops. He takes a second to close his eyes and concentrate on the smells, and the tension across his shoulders relaxes.

'Diplomacy,' the bishop said, making small talk on the drive down. 'Diplomacy is an important thing. Obviously, we must be truthful. Honesty is what we preach. But I think it's fair to say that it is not always the best thing for the public to know everything.'

Nodding at this point seemed like an appropriate response.

'Too much information, like too much choice, is not necessarily a good thing. We have to consider the level of education of the congregation, even their breadth of experience,' the bishop continued. 'That is part of our duty of care.'

The car sped on, the new polished leather seats a little slippery on the corners. They both maintained a tight grip on the door handles to stop them colliding with one another.

'For example, it was unfortunate that so much was discussed in public about your last post, and perhaps given a slant that was more indicative of the public's desire for gossip rather than the realities of the situation. It can be so damaging to a career of one so young as yourself.' The bishop peered at him through bushy grey eyebrows.

Savvas liked that. And it was true: the press only dwelt on the negative side of the whole affair. After all, everything he had done was for the good of the church. If those reporters had attended his services, they would have heard for themselves how distracting the low-flying planes were. Their racket made contemplation and prayer a difficult matter and interrupted his sermons to the point where he was obliged to stop and wait for the rumbling to pass and the echoes within the church to subside before he could continue. Why his predecessor had not raised money to insulate against the noise when the airport first opened was a mystery.

'I can see how the amount you raised could have been questioned and I think, if there ever was a next time, perhaps a little keeping of receipts, a little accounting for expenditure might help.'

That enraged him. Was the bishop suggesting he had pocketed the funds? Surely he must know that a papas as young as himself will only be treated with respect if he respects himself. He is a representative of God. It is imperative that he must, at all times, be smart and well-groomed, manicured and coiffured. How else will the congregation set him apart, recognise his stature? He must live his role wholeheartedly and also, he must keep a well-stocked kitchen to ensure that he is in a position to offer his hospitality at any given moment to bishops and archdeacons, should they call round. All that costs money. There is no getting around the realities of life, no matter how spiritual one becomes.

'But,' the bishop continued, 'the church can always do with good active men and of course I am not only talking financially, my dear Savvas. Take your new position, for example.'

His ears pricked up at this point. Not much had been said about where the church was sending him so far. He asked where they were going, but the reply—the name of a town he had never heard of—meant nothing to him, and he did not want to admit his ignorance. His knowledge of Greek geography is poor, and it embarrassed him. Besides, after the reports in the tabloids, he was given very little choice. Also, returning to Greece would have fulfilled his mama's dream for him. But returning to where? They had already driven for over an hour out of Athens, and the roads were practically deserted, the low houses made of *plythra*, the rendered mud-brick conspicuous by its rounded corners. There was scrubland on either side, and, occasionally, the sound of goat bells. At intervals along the roadside, orange sellers sat with their carrier bags full of the fruits, hoping to tempt the passing drivers. They were heading into a social wilderness.

Returning his attention to the cooking, he stirs the onions, which are now translucent, and the sweet aroma of garlic begins to make his new kitchen smell more like home. Even if it is a rather small home. The pine nuts and the rice are stirred in next. Normally, he would add the meat at this stage but as there was none in the fridge when he arrived, this version will have to be with raisins. An extra spoonful of the kernels will make up for the beef.

How pleased his mama would have been for him to end up in such a remote location, he is not sure. He can hear her now:

'Make me proud, Savvas. Make your baba proud.' She talked with such authority, both for herself and for his baba, who died when he was six years old. He only really knew his baba through her but she assured him, at six feet four, he was even more to reason with than her.

Which was hard to imagine. His teen years, without a male role model, were a difficult time; confusing, full of unanswered questions.

'Have dignity, stay close to God, and never turn your back on who you are,' were his mama's instructions when he struggled with questions of what his life was all about in the days before leaving school. 'Above all, you are Greek, Savvas. Be proud of that!'

Her ambitions for him felt so lofty and then, towards her end, so hurried. There was no time for contemplative thought. She suggested he become a priest, and a priest he became. How proud she was, lying in her bed, the white sheets neatly tucked in, the pointless jug of water by her side, her parched lips cracking into a strained smile as she stared at the pictures of him outside the church, ordained. She looked at that picture so long, her weakened fingers struggling to maintain a grip, and eventually it slipped to the bedspread and then to the floor. As he picked it up, he saw there were tears in her eyes and she whispered, 'So proud.'

He dabs his eyes with the edge of his apron. The onions must be making his eyes water.

Would being in Greece have been enough for her, no matter how lowly the station, or should he have challenged the wisdom of the church to demand he remain in America? He could have waited for a more stately position.

Too late now. It's done.

The oven door needs a little brute force to get it to open, but the inside has heated quickly. Perhaps he needs to turn down the temperature a little. An extra sprinkle of breadcrumbs to keep the tops from burning might be enough.

The *tapsi* of stuffed tomatoes, surrounded by potatoes and liberally coated with olive oil, is now ready to slide into the oven. This is going to be a good meal. A private housewarming for one. He takes a glass from the overhead cupboard and checks it for finger marks and is surprised to find it is spotless.

A glass of wine accompanies him to the adjacent room, where he slumps into the chair by the open fire. The chair is not uncomfortable, but for a man of the church to live in two rooms—one to cook and eat in and one to sleep in—what does that say to the people? He will definitely have to do something about that. He smooths his beard, which is coming along quite well now, and adjusts the knot of his ponytail at the back so it does not dig into his neck as he rests back.

Pinching finger and thumb, he picks tiny flecks of dirt from his floor-length black cassock before sipping his wine, looking around the room.

In places, the greying plaster is crumbling to dust and falling off the wall. Where the door handle has hit against the wall is a deep gouge, and along the bottoms of the walls, in corners where small insects have burrowed, there are tiny mounds of red earth from their tunnels in the mud brick. These areas will need attention. There are no drapes hanging at the two small windows, which gives the room a bare feeling. The dark wood, half-glass-fronted kitchen crockery cabinet by the main door is the only item with any ornamentation, but even this is drab. A table for one up against the wall also supports the countertop stove in which his *tapsi* of stuffed tomatoes bubbles away. All in all, it won't do.

Through the window by the table, all that can be seen is the solid, blank back of the square-cut grey stone church. An impenetrable sun shield. The spring warmth is in the air outside, but it has yet to penetrate this hovel. The flames lick up the back of the chimney, drawing him closer, mesmerising.

'Take your new position…' the bishop said in the car on the way from the airport. 'Your predecessor was a good man. A very good man.

But perhaps…' He paused and looked out the window then, as if lost in thought before resuming, 'Perhaps too good a man.'

It wasn't the comment that intrigued Savvas, it was something that the bishop left unspoken that caught his attention. The pause, the sigh, the lack of explanation.

'How can that be?' He asked the question directly.

'Ah, well…' He could sense rather than see the man's cheeks take on a ruddier colour. The bishop cleared his throat nervously. 'It is true that we must walk the way of Christ.' His voice was quiet, humble. 'There can be no argument with that.' He shook and then nodded to emphasise this point, but he could not make eye contact. Savvas waited. The silence in the air between them, pressuring the bishop to account for his unspoken comment, the rumble of the tyres against tarmac seemed louder. The older man nervously glanced at the chauffeur, whose eyes were fixed on the road ahead.

Savvas bowed his head as if in agreement and, leaning in, created the impression of intimacy.

'It is just that sometimes…' the Bishop reduced his tone to a whisper. 'Sometimes a man can be so humble, it does him no favours.'

'Yes, yes, how right you are,' Savvas murmured. 'And my predecessor was such a man, you suspect, Bishop?'

'Suspect? I know. The house attached to the church in this village...'

At this point, Savvas looked up and sharply. A village! No one had said anything to him about a village! A tiny Greek peasant village over an hour from Athens! He was about to speak out when the bishop continued, 'It is a rather grand house.'

This refocused Savvas and for the moment, he held his tongue.

'A wide hallway, chandeliers, rather a fine dining room, a large balcony at the front and a small but maintainable garden at the rear.' The old man had smoothed his black robes over his knee with his free hand.

So it seemed it was just as well he had held his tongue. Maybe the place would suit him. A nice house and a small parish. It could be a good start.

'Well.' The bishop leaned even closer to Savvas. 'He gave it away,' he hissed though his teeth.

'What?' Savvas sat upright. The driver glanced through the rearview mirror at this, making the briefest of eye contact.

'Yes.' The bishop kept his head bowed over his knees, trying to maintain his hushed tone. 'His argument was that a single old man had no need of such space and luxury. Whereas his housekeeper, with her gardener husband, who, when they were not serving on him and maintaining the church, lived with their daughter in a two-room cottage. So he swapped.'

Savvas swallowed and shut his mouth at that point, not trusting himself to speak.

Pouring a second glass of wine, he stands and walks the two paces to check on his dinner. The smell is most appetising but the tops are definitely going to burn unless he turns the heat down. His stomach twists. He has not eaten since the light lunch he had with the bishop in nearby Saros town, after which the chauffeur drove them directly to the village.

On that brief journey, the bishop hurriedly informed him that the gardener, since the bestowal of the house, had passed away. Or did he pass away before? It was not entirely clear. Either way, it seemed the housekeeper and her daughter were now installed in the larger house.

'The widow took up the burden of the gardening as well as the housekeeping and church duties,' the bishop explained.

Savvas was about to enquire of the duties of the widow as regards his own domestic comfort such as the laundry and cleaning when the bishop continued.

'But it was too much for her, poor woman. No one knows how long she laid unable to move on the cold marble floor by the altar. She had a second stroke six months later and now is confined to a chair.'

Savvas wondered then to what kind of place he was being taken. The *papas* in a small village house, his immobile housekeeper in her grand house unable to perform the least of her duties. It seemed there was a lot to do to straighten things out.

'But I think you will find the daughter keeps everything well now,' the bishop assured him.

'When you say my predecessor gave them the house, you mean he let them use it or…' But his question hung unfinished as the driver pulled up to what was indeed a very fine-looking house with an open vista next to a rather small and uncared-for cottage tucked behind the church. Between the two stood an old-fashioned well with boards covering it and flowers in olive oil tin pots displayed on top. Someone had painted the tins in bright colours.

That was a couple of hours ago. The bishop rapped on the door of the grand house until it opened a crack, closed again and reopened, and something was handed over. The old man adjusted his *kalimavkion,* which a slight breeze was trying to pluck from his head, as he made his way back to the car.

'Nefeli apologises. She cannot come out to greet you as she is just feeding her mama, but she assures me that the house has been prepared and the larder stocked.' With a gracious movement, the bishop opened the car door and invited him out. 'I think perhaps it is really her shyness that has kept her indoors.' This last sentence was said with a wisp of a smile, as if offering some joviality into a situation that was clearly, through Savvas' eyes, far from amusing.

He had never before stood in front of any building so basic with the intention of entering. The tool shed behind his old church in America was just a breeze block affair, but even that had a sense of purpose. This greying squat cottage looked very much like it had grown, beginning life, perhaps, as a wall, then a second wall added at an angle to become a sheep enclosure, maybe. It would be easy to imagine that a roof was added to turn it into a donkey shed but how, from that, anyone had had the vision to make it a house is beyond imagination! Words stuck in his throat. He was rendered speechless. As he stumbled to untangle the priority of his feelings, the bishop used the pause to put the keys in his hand and, more quickly than he could have ever anticipated, the old man wished him well and jumped back in the car, leaving him standing there in the dusk, alone.

His dinner is beginning to burn. He can smell it. He has always had a very delicate sense of smell. If he was a proud man, which of course he isn't, he would be proud of his sense of smell.

The stuffed tomato tops are browned but not blackened, the skins softened and collapsing like old feather pillows. The tray of food is hot and he is not about to use the edge of his new outer cassock, which he still has not removed, to take the tomatoes out of the heat. Looking around the room reveals nothing useful. From previous exploration, he knows that one side of the lower cupboard of the kitchen crockery cabinet is stacked with plates and jugs to keep them dust free, and the other side is stocked with basic dried foodstuffs. The tomatoes were in the fridge with other basics. At least the housekeeper seems to know her job.

But right now he needs a towel or a cloth, and she's overlooked that.

A narrow door next to the china cabinet opens into a small wet room. This has been built onto the older stone house with breeze blocks, their outlines still visible under a thin coat of white paint. With a shudder at the thought of showering there, he snatches the towel from the rail and returns to save his dinner. The towel smells of damp.

The flavours are good, the rice perhaps a little dry, but the tomato shells themselves are exquisite with the butter, especially if he scoops into each mouthful a good quantity of pine nuts. He swills this eagerly anticipated food down with two more glasses of wine, puts the empty plate on the floor, and lays back in his chair, his hand across his extended stomach.

This is the moment in the day he most looks forward to. Work done, a good meal inside him, the door to the outside world shut. True, there is much to do, both on the small scale of unpacking his bags and boxes and also on the larger scale of sorting out where he will live long term. But right now, he is content.

Well, almost content. Lurching to his feet, he shuffles to the fridge. Yes, he thought so, a tub of *rizogalo*, sweet rice pudding, and if he was not mistaken, yes, a carton of condensed milk. The two are soon combined into one bowl with a few spoonfuls of soft brown sugar and he returns to his seat with what is left of the bottle of wine.

As he spoons the sweet, creamy contents into his mouth, his already-full stomach feels like it is about to burst. Licking his lips, he wipes his mouth on the back of his hand. There is a small irritation in the moment when he spies his wine glass on the kitchen table, far too far away to reach at this point in time. Instead, he grabs the wine bottle by its neck and swings it to his lips, drinking the last of the red nectar straight from the bottle. Then his grip loosens and the bottle clatters into his now-empty bowl on the floor and he stretches back for a second time, utterly relaxed. So full now that he is unable to move.

He spends his first night sleeping in the chair, barely able to move.

It is not a noise that wakes him. She is quiet as the proverbial church mouse. Nor is it the morning sun. She must have slipped in, hardly opening the door at all. It is her smell that rouses him. In his dream, he is sleeping, lying on his back on a church pew, and the majestic church ceiling changes colour, becomes green and turns into grass. With it comes the sweet smell of the outdoors, a trace of jasmine, a hint of ozone, a pinch of pine. He twitches, the dream fades. Surfacing slowly, he rubs his nose, opens one eye and, unaware of her presence, stumbles to his feet, hands outstretched to feel his way to the bathroom where he urinates and relieves the pressure of the gases that have built up in his gut overnight. It makes him groan with relief and, tucking himself back in, he returns to the main room, lowering his cassock.

'Oh my God, who the? How the?' First, his gaze is fixed on her, her extraordinary colouring, then he looks to the front door, which he is certain he locked last night.

She continues to dry the pots she must have washed whilst he was asleep. Heat stings his cheeks; he flushes to his forehead, aware of his performance in the bathroom only seconds before.

'Must you do that now?' It is all he can think to say. He wants to be alone, wake up slowly, come to terms with where he is. He looks around the small room to remind himself of his new situation. In the grim light of morning, it all looks worse, if that were possible. He will almost certainly need to spend the day composing a letter to explain why this is not the ideal situation for him. Athens, after all, is huge. There must be a position there, even if it is in a poor area. He can do that, work with the deprived.

The girl drying the pots doesn't answer but under her long fringe, he can see her pupils have grown wider, her movements have frozen, like a startled rabbit. Her eyes are strange. She is what he has always considered to be a Greek throwback. From when he was a small boy, he has heard the rumours that the Greeks were all blonde before the Arabs made their way across the water. Her hair is not blond exactly, rather a light brown, a dirty blond perhaps, but her eyes are such a pale brown, they are almost green and it is not clear to him if she is wearing makeup or the lashes around her eyes are just dense and dark. And there's that smell again. It was not a dream. It is her.

She puts down the cloth she is using to dry his dishes and with a bowed head and light feet, she is at the door.

'Sorry, no, that was rude of me.' Savvas controls himself. 'Please do not go. You are doing a fine job.' That's better. He is not a savage and probably has more manners than this whole village put together. She stops, motionless, fingers entwined in front of her, head bowed a little and her fringe all but hiding her face. Her eyes dart this way and that, unsure of what she should do next.

'I think you were dealing with your mama when I arrived yesterday; we were not introduced. Your name is?' He holds out his hand, ready to shake hers. She turns to face him, which stirs the air, the smell of her, fresh linen, jasmine, and sweetness growing stronger for a second. Her hand extends and he takes it to shake but almost draws his own back when his palm chafes against her callused skin.

'Nefeli,' she says. Her voice is neither loud nor soft, but somehow it has a still quality. Her pale eyes are set on his left ear, not making eye contact. She seems not to want to let him in. After a second, it is her hand that is the first to retract and he realises that perhaps he has fallen into a stare and held on too long. Then she bends her knee and is crouched by his feet. This action is completely out of his range of experience. Is she bowing to him? Does she want to kiss his hand like he is the patriarch or something? Should he ask her to rise? It is very flattering, such uncompromising subjection, but now that she is at his feet, he is not sure what to do. Her head goes lower. Surely she is not expecting to kiss his feet?

'Please, arise,' are all the words he can find to say. At this point, her arm stretches out by the side of his foot and it is only when she stands with the empty wine bottle in her hand that he realises his mistake. It must have rolled half under the chair when he was sleeping. She wasn't genuflecting; she was tidying up his mess.

Face to face again, her eyes dart at him under her dirty blond curtain.

'Do you want me to cook?' she asks.

Again, she has confused him. It is first thing in the morning. A coffee would be nice, and a slice of cake perhaps but, oh yes, of course, she must mean later.

'Actually, I like to cook, myself. But if I have a very busy schedule, you could ready me a light lunch mid-afternoon: some cold meats, a salad, something of a dessert, that sort of thing.'

'Busy?' At least, that is what he thinks she says. She glances around the room, picks up the wet towel she was drying the pots with and, wine bottle in her other hand, she lets herself out.

Two, maybe three minutes is all the conversation has taken. He stares blankly at the back of the door. It didn't go as he envisaged his first meeting with his housekeeper. He intended to talk about the grand house, find out if her living there with her mama was just a casual solution that was given to them in the moment by his predecessor, or whether it was something more formal. He also needs more information as to the running of things. What days will she do his laundry, for example, and does she have a day off in the month or not? If not, he could bestow one on her. That would be a good beginning. Also, he could have found out a little about his congregation from her. Are they all farmers here or is there another source of work? In the village square, they passed a *kafeneio*, a corner shop, a bakery, an eatery. Is there more tucked behind on the side streets?

But instead of using the situation to his own advantage, he stood there and shook her hand and stared. And why on earth did he imagine that she was curtseying to him?

It isn't often he is glad his mama is not around but right now, he is very relieved that she is not there to witness his crassness.

It was the girl's eyes, the darkness around them as if she hadn't washed, the lightness of the irises, and her smell.

Somewhere in the village, a cockerel crows and a second one, further away, fainter, competes. It serves to remind him how far he is from civilisation. There is a chance, but he does not hold much hope with this thought, that this parochial cluster of inhabitance will look better under the powerful spring sun than it did in the dusk of the night before. Which reminds him he must tell Nefeli that one of her duties will be to open the shutters around this cottage each morning, just until the mix-up with the grand house is sorted out. Coffee by eight o'clock and breakfast by nine. Best to keep her busy. Mama taught him well on that premise, and he was never allowed to be idle.

The front door catches on a floor tile that is lifted at one corner. He rocks it flat with his toe and the door swings open easily. He dips his head under the door's crossbeam so as not to hit his tall black *kalimavkion*. Unlike his last one, this new one is a perfect fit, so it is worth taking a bit of care. All of a sudden, there is a smell of sheep and someone, not too far away, is cooking: tomatoes, onions, and oregano.

The grey blank wall of the church is not a welcoming sight. He looks longingly to the proper house alongside him, the sun's rays bathing it in light. The whitewashed stonework could do with being freshened up, but the shutters have been recently painted. The first floor balcony basks in glorious sunshine. How much easier it is to praise God when you live in wonderful surroundings. He will breakfast on that balcony. The girl and her mama are bound to be happier in the cottage, playing out their own small lives, and each morning, with such a place to have coffee and cake, he will praise God indeed.

He looks around for the garage, but there does not appear to be one. How is he expected to get in and out of the village, go to Saros, attend church meetings in Athens if they have not allocated him a car?

As he steps out from the end of the church wall, the sun falls on his face. Closing his eyes, he reminds himself to be thankful for the little pleasures such as this. Around the front of the church is a large paved area on which, despite the early hour, three boys are kicking around a ball. With the sun's heat warming his face, the boys calling for the ball, and a smell of home cooking, the overall effect is very seductive.

No, he is not ready for that yet. There will be time enough to get involved with the people of the village, to relax. First, he must deal with business and at the top of the agenda is securing a car. Unless he is mistaken, he spotted a bureau in the bedroom last night. He must make a list of repairs that need doing, improvements required in the bathroom if he is to stay here, things that the cottage is short of, and then he will take the morning to write the appropriate letters. He will also jot down a few notes for his Sunday reflections that seem to go down well after the service. He turns to go back to his cottage.

'Welcome, welcome,' a voice calls to him. Opposite the church, a woman is sweeping the road in front of her house. It is much like his own cottage but hers looks happier somehow. Geraniums burst out of pots propped on the wall; a cat is rubbing its face against her gate post. A bougainvillea climbs up a post and across some supports, framing her front door which is wide open, releasing the smells of cooking. His mama was the same. She never got out of the habit of cooking their main meal first thing in the morning, leaving it to keep warm all day in the oven. When he was old enough to be curious and asked why, she replied it was just how she did things 'back home.' 'Cook before it gets too hot to move,' she explained.

The woman brushing the street seems to expect nothing in return for her calls of welcome. Her onions smell like they could be burning. The cat by her gate jumps on the wall and weaves its way between the pots towards her as she sweeps the dust of the road away from her patch. Even this early in the morning, the sun is already strong, penetrating his cassock. He must take his outer cassock off before he starts to sweat.

On the balcony of the grand house, the girl, Nefeli, is hanging washing. The structural arch frames her like a picture and her hair is gold in the sun, all traces of the dirty colour gone. Her lean arms stretch up to hang something white, her gold mane cascading down her back. Each movement is one of strength but she moves with such smooth liquidity that it is possible to imagine she does not disturb the air around her.

'Nefeli.' The voice is right beside him. She leans on her broom, the cat at her ankles. 'Your housekeeper, have you not been introduced yet?'

'Briefly.' Savvas breaks his stare.

'Such a shame.' The woman head rocks from side to side. 'She was lovely when she was tiny but then she had that fall, banged her head. They say it is the scar on her forehead that makes her shy. But I am not fooled by those sly looks of hers. There is no shyness! There is cunning and manipulation. If you value your life at all, do not trust her.' Savvas turns abruptly, unable to believe what he is hearing. The woman does not look mad or vindictive. She smiles warmly at him. 'Losing her baba affected her badly.'

Savvas hesitates. It is not a conversation that he wants to enter. It is one thing to learn about his congregation and quite another to idly gossip, especially when what is being said is so inflammatory. His duty is to diffuse the situation. Yes, that is his duty.

'I know what it is to lose your baba.' He tries to remain aloof and dignified.

'Girls like her should be married,' the woman continues. 'Giving her sultry looks to all and sundry. Your poor predecessor, how could he manage? But who would have her as a wife? She hardly speaks, a crippled mother, and that house has no land you know, not like the cottage. Anyway, I mustn't keep you from all your work. If you need anything Papa, I am Maria. I live there.' She points and then bends her knees, another person at his feet! But she stands, holding the cat.

'Kalimera,' she wishes him and, clutching the cat, the brush held out like a baton in front of her, marches back inside her house.

Nefeli is gone from the balcony. The white washing hangs limply on the line. A football comes flying towards him and only a quick side-step saves his cassock from a dusty imprint.

'Here, Papa, kick it here,' one boy shouts.

'No, over here, Papa.'

He has no intention of kicking the ball anywhere, and he senses the boys are surprised that he is not joining in, which makes him wonder about his predecessor. With a last glance at the balcony, he returns to the cottage.

Closing the door behind him affords space for him to breathe. On the one hand, the robes he wears give him status in the world, the pride and dignity that his mama so wished for him, a credibility seldom offered to one so young. On the other hand, there is no reprieve. Instead, there is a constant demand from others, whether just for a chat or for something more intense. As a representative of God, he cannot say no. Right now, everything feels like a burden. He knows the feeling will pass once he gets used to the place. But these are the moments he misses his mama the most.

'God, why did you have to take Mama?' he speaks out loud. 'And so quickly.' These last words hang heavy in the air. At the time, it was the right thing to do to rush his ordination forward so he could make his mama proud before she was gone. But as time passes, he is realising to an increasing measure the price he will be paying!

'Here is how it is.' Mama's bishop spoke quietly to him over the bed where his semi-conscious mama lay. 'If you marry now, you can get ordained later. But if you are ordained first, you may never marry.'

'But I have no one to marry now,' he hissed in return.

The bishop shrugged. It was not his rule.

Mama slept on. He would be condemning himself to a lifetime of celibacy and maybe even loneliness just to please her before she died. He was finding abstinence hard in these few weeks of his personal pledge, but a vow for a lifetime? She coughed as he had these thoughts. Big hacking, skeleton-shaking coughs that had brought the nurses running, dials checked, pulse taken, a call through to the doctor. Her face grew white, the coughing subsided, eyes suddenly opening as if she was possessed, wide and startled.

'Savvas,' her dry lips whispered. 'Savvas.'

'Here, Mama. I am here.' He held her hand and leaned in.

'Your baba is here. Make him proud, Savvas.'

The nurse raised her eyebrows as if this kind of delusion was to be expected. But it was enough. She was dying; it was so little to ask.

'We must do the ordination as soon as possible,' he said to Mama's bishop, who responded with a sad look and then he took out his diary to see when it could be done.

Now his mama is gone, he is ordained and stuck in a tiny village in Greece, unmarried and with images playing in his mind of Nefeli in the sunlight, struggling with the wet washing that stuck to her in the slight breeze. Sometimes the worldly temptations are too much.

The aroma of yesterday's dinner lingers and the damp smell is seeping out of the bathroom. This cottage is not a fit place for a priest. The shutters are still closed but the sun must have made its way high into the sky, as slices of light now cut horizontal lines across the room. With nothing but the chair by the fireplace at the far end, the stripes of bright sunlight across the whitewashed walls and floor are accentuated. Bars of light. His own personal prison. However, with images of Nefeli floating in his head, and her only being next door, his cage is not so unpleasant. Just small.

With no conscious thought, his hand finds his loins. Catching himself, he regains self-control. He must do something active if he is to overcome his present urges. Writing his lists and letters will occupy his mind.

There is a knock on the door and then, before he has a chance to answer, it opens.

'Papas, coffee?' Nefeli puts her head around the door. The sun streaming in behind her, the smell of heat and jasmine, clean washing and freshly made bread. She pushes the door a little wider to reveal a loaf of bread wrapped in a clean sheet of tissue paper, straight from the bakery, no doubt. His stomach grumbles, determined not to be ignored. With no word of invitation from him, she comes in, puts the bread down on the table.

'Er, coffee, yes, thank you.' Her presence is not what he needs at this moment.

She takes a small *briki*, large enough for a single cup, from its nail on the wall, and then busies herself laying out a cup, saucer, the bread, and a jar of honey. Her movements are too fluid, hypnotising, seductive, and he cannot watch. The best course of action must be to vacate the room until she has finished. He lifts the latch to the bedroom, where the sun streams in through the slatted shutters here too and, once the door is firmly closed behind him, finally, he takes off his outer cassock and looks for a hanger. There are hooks inside the narrow wooden wardrobe and hooks on the back of the door. There is no choice but to lay his robe out on the bed. That will be the first thing on his list. Coat hangers.

The bureau is locked and he fingers the small bunch of keys the bishop gave him last night until he finds the only one that might fit.

The flap drops down to form a writing desk, letting out a faint smell of old books and warm dust. Inside is a mess of papers, and it seems odd that no one from the church has cleared the bureau out already, gone through whatever is there, sorted out his predecessor's personal effects. At the back are slotted compartments, stuffed full of papers, overflowing.

There are stacks of letters about official church business, a collection of newspaper cuttings and a book by the poet Yorgos Seferis. He levers this out and as he does, it falls open at a well-thumbed page. The poem is entitled 'Denial.' The muscle in his thumb tenses, ready to snap the book shut when he sees in faint writing, erased pencil perhaps, the name *Nefeli*. It is written beside a line of the poem that reads 'We wrote her name.' He starts at the top and reads the whole poem. The final verse he whispers out loud:

'With what spirit, what heart, what desire and passion we lived our lives: a mistake. So we changed our life.' The last line is underlined.

He exhales and snaps the book shut. That sort of thing, encouraging feelings and emotions, is exactly what leads to trouble. What sort of man was his predecessor? He drops the book in the empty bin by the bureau and focuses on sorting through the papers. The occasional noise of Nefeli readying his breakfast drifts from the other room and he concentrates with greater earnest.

The first few letters are concerned with mundane church business and tell him nothing other than that his predecessor's first name was Sotos. There is a bill for the covering over of the well, dated eighteen years ago. Why would Sotos keep that? It joins the book in the bin. A letter from a widow informing his predecessor that she will leave all her wealth to the church if he can promise her a place in heaven. This is something he has been told is common enough, but not something he has experienced personally until now. But there is bound to be a whole generation of old people in such rural villages as this. How many confessions, repentances, and accompanying gifts could he gain for the church? He could drop the idea of leaving a portion of their wealth to the church in his after-service thoughts every now and then, keep it fresh in their minds. There are many ways in which he can make his mark in the church, and this could be an easy one. Better to leave one's property to God, he reasons, than to squabbling relatives. All too often, disputes occur when property is passed on and it's not unusual to see houses decay and slowly fall apart because the heirs cannot agree.

Next is a newspaper cutting, its title missing. In fact, the whole of the first column is missing, but the subject is the church. Some of the clippings have yellowed with age, but this one looks fresh. It states that the ten thousand priests and bishops are not paid for by the church but by the state. Well, he didn't know that. He reads on. The new government is trying to alter the law that exempts the church from paying property tax, which the writer of the article declares is shameless, as the church is worth over a billion euros. In the list of properties, there is no mention made of the four hundred and fifty monasteries that were cited in a recent memorandum that was sent round within the church. Maybe that is a good thing. As his new bishop said, it is not always best for the public to know everything. But then the article does go on to say that the Church is the second largest land owner in Greece after the state and holds a significant share in the National Bank of Greece. It says something about the church looking for a billion pounds of investment to build solar farms on the land they own to capitalise on their assets. He would like to be a part of that. That kind of wheeling and dealing excites him. The article summarises that all that has been previously mentioned does not include the eighty bishoprics and their own personal assets, 'which they enjoy with considerable independence.'

'Eighty bishoprics and their own personal assets, which they enjoy with considerable independence,' he reads again, muttering the words whilst hardly moving his lips.

Maybe a bishopric in Greece could suit him. It sounds as if they have more freedom here than in America.

There is a tap at the door.

'Okay.' Savvas lets her know he has heard. Then everything stops. The news clipping falls from his hands. His breathing quickens slightly. There it is! A rubber-stamped document that seems to be the official transfer of the grand house to two named people. The last name is Nefeli. How fortuitous it is that he has found it so easily. Mind you, there is very little else in the desk. His predecessor can't have been very active with regards to raising funds for the church. But even so. He must take his time to read it, decipher the small print that is written in tedious legal terms. He must find out exactly how official it is and whether there is room for some manoeuvre. If he got the house back for the church, that would be a boost to his position in the church's eyes and it would surely be an asset if he sets his course toward a bishopric. With a bounce in his step, he goes to enjoy his breakfast.

Nefeli has moved the table from up against the wall to the centre of the room and there is a vase of delicate bluey-purple flowers in the centre. She has opened the shutters and a square of sunshine highlights all she has laid out for his breakfast. There is a smell of fresh bread and toast, coffee and, again, jasmine. With grace, she steps toward the door as he sits.

'If I might have a word before you go.' The way she looks from under her fringe stirs him, as if she is holding back a secret—or sharing one; he is not sure. It feels intimate even though she probably wears her hair that way to keep the world out. 'Please, take a seat.' He notes that the coffee in his small coffee cup glistens on top with tiny bubbles, no grounds to be seen. It pleases him. She sits perched on the chair's edge as if ready to take flight.

'How is your mother?' It's a safe opening that shows the right degree of concern. He waits, but she does not answer. Maybe it is more than shyness. Perhaps she is not all there. She doesn't twitch or flex as she sits there, motionless. The curve of her neck down into her back, nipping in at her waist, is highlighted by the sun's rays.

'Good, good.' Savvas breaks the silence. 'Have you lived here all your life?' She flinches at this.

'I don't live here, I live there.' She turns her face in the direction of the grand house.

'No. I mean…'

'I used to live here,' she adds. It catches Savvas off guard. He had not expected her to speak without being prompted by a specific question.

'Did you like it when you lived here?' It might be a good question or it might be entirely the wrong question. What if she hated it in the cottage?

'I used to play in the olive grove behind and around the well until I fell…'

'Ah yes, I heard you banged your head.'

'Down the well.'

Savvas stops buttering his toast and looks up at her.

'Sorry.' But he thinks he has understood. 'You fell down the well?'

'Yes.'

'Good grief. Was it deep?' He is trying to make out how badly her forehead is scarred, but too much of her dirty golden hair falls over her face. Her chin nods down and to one side and she consciously blinks. A very Greek unspoken yes.

'Mother of God, you must have seen stars.' He bestows a smile on her but it is not returned.

The glance she casts him is hard and cold as if he has just accused her of something. She is certainly not an easy person to talk to.

'Well, I am glad you are alright.' Where was he? What was he saying to her? Oh yes, trying to find out if she liked the cottage. Well, if she fell and bumped her head, maybe this is not the best tactic. He will try another.

'Do you find the house you are in now a little big to maintain on your own?'

Her accusing looks softens and her fingers relax in her lap. Such long fingers. Like her limbs, long and graceful.

'I am very grateful. It assures Mama a home whilst she is alive.'

The words fall like music to his ears. If she is right, the house is only theirs until her mama's death. That could give him possibilities. God is smiling on him.

'Yes, I am sure you are.' Now, he mustn't rush this. Play it carefully, first make her realise that he is looking out for her, build some trust. Then, when he has a plan, she will go along with his wishes. After all, it will be for her own good as well as for the good of the church.

'By the way, I meant to ask, is it possible for you to do my laundry?' Diplomatic tactics. The laundry is part of her job description but he read in some magazine, years ago, that people trust other people not through flattery and gifts but by finding that they offer to do things for them. The article said that the logic is they would not have offered to do something for someone they didn't trust, so, therefore, they conclude they must trust the person.

'Fridays,' she replies without feeling. It seems the trust thing will take time to sink in. Perhaps now he should back it up by offering her something in return.

'And do you take days off?' He tries to make it sound like a light enquiry.

This question seems to baffle her. 'No.' The word is cautious, as if the question is some trick.

'Then I suggest you take a day off a month. How would that be?' She is bound to be grateful.

'And who will look after Mama on that day?'

'Oh, I see. No, I meant a day off from your housekeeping duties.' But she does not seem pleased, not even grateful, just another nod, lead with her chin, agreed with by a blink of her eyes.

'Is that all?' She stands.

'Yes.' Savvas thinks about asking for more coffee. Something about the awkwardness between them repels him but as she stands, the way she moves suddenly inflames him. It is nothing she does intentionally. Rather, it is the way one of her knees rounds the other as she stands, the way her hips settle, ready to move. She is like an animal, a fragile animal with callused palms from hard work. She leaves.

Once she is gone, he stares towards the light. The back windows look out over an olive grove, no blank church wall there. With the shutters closed, he had not realised how rural the cottage is at the rear, opening onto trees and more trees. He can imagine Nefeli as a small child running between them, her hair flowing behind her, her long limbs speeding her flight. Then to fall down a well... How scared she must have been. How long was she down there? That sort of experience is enough to make anyone feel the world is an unsafe place.

A flick of a memory demands his attention. The hours he spent lying in the crucifix position on the cold church floor in penance for some wrong he had done. His mama on her knees, praying for his seven-year-old soul. His baba so recently dead to the world. Everything cold. The floor cold, his mama cold in her heart, his baba cold in his grave. Cold.

He involuntarily shivers. He can understand Nefeli's reserve, how easy it would have been for him to have taken that course, to have retreated inside himself, allowing his mama and the bullies at school to win. It was the softness and the concern of his mama's priest that made the difference. He showed concern, compassion, offered support. Time and time again, he has sat in the sanctuary of the priest's quarters reading the bible. Not because he wanted to read the bible but because that was what was expected of him when he sought refuge there and it seemed to please the priest. He sought the peace of those walls so often that one day, he found he had learnt some of the scriptures so well, he could quote them. The first time these pleasant passages came to his tongue unrequested was against his Mama. That shocked him. She accused him of something which he had not done and out popped a quotation: 'Let him with no sin cast the first stone.'

Her face went white, her fists clenched, and she looked like she was going to explode. In response, his own legs tensed, ready to run. But the outburst he was expecting from her never came. Her tension uncoiled, her colour returned, and she muttered something that almost sounded like an apology. It gave him such a feeling of power, so he tried the same tactic to defend himself against the school ruffians. With Biblical quotes, he pointed out the errors of their ways, promising eternal Hell for their actions. To his surprise, they didn't laugh. Instead, it seemed his words scared them.

Very soon, his position in life changed dramatically. His relationship with his mama became more equal, although she was still ever hard to please. He became someone who was respected at school. The teachers treated him with something approaching reverence. The only negative was from the priest who had showed him concern and support in the first place. He backed away as Savva's confidence and arsenal of quotes grew. This was a response which Savvas struggled to understand. But to counteract the negative effect of losing the priest's blessing, the bishop took him under his wing instead. He became a soldier of God.

Through in the bedroom, he pulls up the wooden chair to sit at the desk. The legs scrape across the floor, inscribing their mark in the layer of settled dust. The raffia seat is coming undone, something else that needs mentioning.

The officially stamped paper lays uppermost, Nefeli's clearly marked.

He will read it through, focus his attention on getting into the big house. Then all this list writing and complaining about petty things like raffia chairs will be unnecessary. The book in the wastepaper bin catches his eye, and he finds himself retrieving it, the rhythm of the poem calling to his senses. Reading it over this time, it is the first verse that hits him hardest.

'On the secret seashore, white like a pigeon we thirst at noon, but the water was brackish.' He is not totally clear what it means, but it resonates. He thirsts but the water is brackish. That's how he feels; driven by something like thirst, but the water he is offered is not clear, not pure.

No, this thinking is self-indulgent nonsense. It is all emotional drivel.

He pulls out the bill for covering over the well, which has stuck between the book's final pages. Presumably Sotos had that done after

Nefeli's fall. If he had been here at the time he would have poured a truckload of concrete down it, sealed it forever, not just boarded it over with a piece of wood.

His mind is wandering again. Where was he? Oh yes, the official paper for the big house.

Head bowed, he concentrates, glad now that his mama spoke only Greek at home, although this document is mostly in official Greek, which seems more like ancient Greek, and despite his fluency, he struggles.

'Ah. I see!' It is not such good news. The two people named—Nefeli and her crippled mama—have official rights to the house for their lifetimes. They do not own the house, but they have legal possession of it. But that could be, well, potentially, his lifetime. That's bad.

He looks up and stares at the blank wall. If he keeps in mind that Nefeli thinks she only has the place until her mama's death, he must be able to work it to his advantage somehow. Perhaps if he offers her something more permanent for herself, she might give up the big house before her mama dies.

His gaze drops to the wooden floor.

Perhaps it is better if she never knows the house could be hers for her lifetime. As the bishop said, it is sometimes better that people do not know everything.

A tap at the front door rouses him. Looking at his Rolex (a gift to himself to celebrate the completion of the noise insulation on his church in America), he wonders why Nefeli would be back so soon. It is nowhere near lunchtime. Leaving the papers on the desk, he goes through to let her in, but it is not Nefeli.

'Ah, er.' He cannot remember her name.

'Maria,' she prompts. He hadn't really taken note of her before. She is thinner than she appeared in her housecoat, sweeping the road outside her house, perhaps even on the skinny, malnourished side. She must be late middle age because her hair is a flat dark colour that only a bottle of dye can bring. In front of her ears, the roots flash grey.

'Can I help you?' He would like to continue with his thoughts, sort through more of the papers.

'Yes, you can. Someone stole my bike a couple of weeks ago and no one has done a thing about it and then some items of clothing went from my washing line and I suspect it is the same boys, but there is no discipline these days, they run amuck, playing football when they should be at school and stealing peoples' property.'

The last thing he wants to do is invite her in, but to stand talking on the doorstep is inappropriate.

'Shall we go over to the church?' He steps out into the sunshine, looks up. It is surprisingly hot. One minute spring, the next summer.

'No, Papas. The last papas offered some reflections after the Sunday service. It's not traditional, but I know how you priests like the sound of your own voices. Here.' She thrusts a sheet of paper at him, which he gingerly accepts. 'I have provided you with some material for these reflections, best to give these young criminals' families a bit of a nudge about their responsibilities.'

'Thank you for your efforts, but I tend to write my own sermons, Kyria Maria.' He pushes the papers back to her but she withdraws her hand. He all but prods her in her stomach with them.

'You are new here, Papas. There are many things to learn about our village. One thing I know, and I am passing it on to you, is that there needs to be more self-discipline around here.'

He has seen this before in his parish in America, where there was a woman called Janet-

Lee. Every week, she would have some grievance with someone and she would find their faults, write them up as a sermon without directly mentioning any names, and then deliver it to him to be read on Sundays. The first time she did this, she caught him off guard and he accepted the notes, but on reading them through, it was transparently obvious that vengeance was the motive and it was clear to whom she was referring. He burnt those notes in the fire. They felt potentially explosive. But having accepted them once, Janet-Lee seemed to think this was all the permission she needed to do it every week. Each essay, he put straight on the fire at home. But about two months later, in a quiet, almost bored moment when he had just received the news that his application for a grant to insulate the church had been turned down, he flipped though her latest offering and found within some very interesting information about a local council man involved in the processing of grant applications. With the right word in the right place, the grant went through smoothly, with a much larger budget than that for which he had initially applied. After that, he read Janet-Lee's weekly offering avidly. It is amazing what people will do when something becomes personal. But as it is always personal when God is involved—does He not see everything, does He not know everything?—Savvas never felt guilt in using his knowledge in his dealings.

In the end, it could be said the he was just adapting to the ways of the world for the greater glory of the church. After all, God helps those who help themselves. Mama had told him this repeatedly. That was how his baba became the man he was, she said, although Savas was never sure what it was that his baba had done when he was alive. All he knew was that it was enough to keep his mama in comfort and private health care to the end of her days.

Maria does not take back her notes. Instead, she wishes him a good morning, her hands behind her back as she walks away. The same cat he saw earlier that morning follows her as she goes.

The sheaves of paper are covered in a spidery hand-written scrawl. Maybe he will go and find the local kafeneio and read them through, but then he would be sidetracked by meeting everyone, so perhaps not. He hasn't even seen inside the church yet, but a church is a church, and he will be spending much of his future life there, so there is no hurry. However, the walls of the cottage are beginning to feel like they are closing in around him. He needs to get out, but where to go? No car means he is stuck in the village for now. That's the first letter he will write, but for now, he needs to be outside. He goes around to the side of the cottage past the firmly boarded-up well.

The olive grove behind the house is not very big but would provide an income for a small family. He walks between the trees, which do not appear well tended. Did his predecessor take care of them? Did he rent out the land? Or did he leave it in the hands of Nefeli's family? That is most likely.

The sunlight dapples the ground through the olive branches. The breath of an occasional breeze spins the leaves to show the bluey-green flashing to silver, and then back again. The rustling is so soft, he has to focus on it to hear it properly. There is a smell of warm earth and somewhere towards the village, a dog barks and children laugh. A car changes gear behind him and over at the grand house, a shutter bangs as if caught by the slight wind. It is peaceful here. His mama would love that he is Greece, in the land of his roots, in amongst the olive trees. She would be joyous at his coming home.

Below a tree he finds a smooth rock that is almost clear of twigs and debris. He sweeps at it with his foot, then sits. It is clearly a spot others have chosen before him, with the curve of the tree trunk just right to lean against. The view through the trees is a delight, the dappling of sun perfect. When did he last sit like this, on the ground in the sun? Not since he was a boy! He is glad he has two extra cassocks because this may dirty the one he is wearing, but right now, in the moment, he doesn't care about the dust.

He smooths out Maria's essay, which he has curled into a tube, and begins to read. It reads like a person trying to write a sermon as they imagine a priest would write. It is full of clichés and familiar bible quotes. It is all focused on making whoever has stolen her items of clothing feel guilty. Exactly what the items were is not specified. Having quickly read to this point, he is just about to give up when the last few paragraphs seem to change subject. They read, 'even men of the church cannot resist all things.' Is she talking about him or the last papas, Sotos?

'They are just as susceptible to the charms of the devil as any man.' His interest is momentarily aroused. Then it goes on to quote various bible passages that seem to have no relevance until, at the end, underlined: 'Even with a whole heart, even with a whole spirit, desires and passions can take our lives until we realise it is a mistake. Sometimes it is too late to

change our lives.' Savvas frowns, trying to recall
where he has read this. Somewhere, recently.
Yes, isn't that the last verse of the poem
underlined in the book from the bureau? When
would Maria have had access to the papas' inner
chamber?

A tree root is digging into his bottom and he
tries crossing his ankles the other way around,
but it brings no relief. Shuffling to one side, he
looks at the ground to judge where it is flattest.
The tree root arcs out of the soil before returning
underground and reappearing to mould into the
trunk. Where he has been leaning is the only bit
of bark that is smooth. The rest of the tree is
twisted and knotted, with deep holes and
fissures that suggest multiple sapling trunks
have grown and fused together. Some of the
holes are so deep, they are partly filled with
leaves and debris, but something blue is in one
that is at ground level and wide enough for an
animal to live in. Whatever it is has been stuffed
deeply in the hole, leaving only a corner
showing. Rolling onto hands and knees allows
him to see more clearly that it is a book.

He looks around the olive grove, but apart
from the humming of insects, he is alone. The
book sticks as he tries to retrieve it and it takes
bit of wiggling for it to come free. It does not

look old, but when he opens it, on the first page is the date some ten years before. He flips through to the end, where the last date, in a very uncertain hand, is earlier this year. He remembers his own horror when he caught his mama reading his journal, and his initial response is to return the book to its hiding place. But something about the last date and the handwriting cause him to falter.

With another look around the grove, he pulls it free once again and puts the book up his sleeve to return to the cottage.

Just as he steps through his front door into the shadows, a ringing sound emanates from among the bags and boxes that remain untouched where he put them down on his arrival last night. It is his phone. With quick movements, yanking at buckles and pulling harshly on zips, he locates his state-of-the-art mobile. The book in his sleeve is proving an inconvenience and so, hurriedly pulling it out, he puts it in amongst his things. He hurriedly presses the answer button and speaks in a slightly breathless voice.

'Hello?'

'Ah Savvas, how did you sleep?' It is the bishop.

'Yes fine.' He tries to recall the most pressing point he needs to address with the bishop. It returns to him quickly. 'Yes thank you, now I am just finding my feet. But I am having trouble locating my car...'

'Car?' The bishop seems thrown by such a request. 'Do you really think you will need one?'

Savvas can feel a knot of tension start at the base of his neck. He is leaning against the wall and part of the bedroom doorframe digs into his back.

'Well, I really think...'

'Settling in all right?' The bishop's voice is jolly, cheerful, deflecting.

'It's a bit small. I was wondering if…' He pushes off from the frame and turns to pick at the paint that is peeling off the moulding, small flakes falling to the wooden floorboards.

'Is Nefeli taking care of you?'

'Yes, yes.' An image of her squeezes out all logical thought and practical issues. He stops running his nails under the paint. 'Is she, well, can I ask?' He stammers 'The bump on her head, how badly has it affected her?' A voice inside his head qualifies it as a rational question. After all, he needs to know what sort of person he is dealing with, both as his housekeeper and in relation to the house.

'Ah yes, poor child. How scared she must have been. They did not find her immediately. When they brought her up, she was delusional, I heard. She created in her mind a magical world out of the well and they say she never really returned to reality.'

'Magical world?' It rings a bell of recognition for Savvas. How he tried to make his own deceptive reality when lying on the cold church floor in a crucifix position all those times. With his eyes tightly shut, rolling his weight a little to one side so only one leg and half his chest touched the cold tiles, he tried to convince himself that really he was basking on the hot sand on the beach or lounging on a furry rug in front of a fire. As the floor's temperature bit deeper, he tried to just imagine the cold was really heat. Sometimes, he could do that, and it almost felt like he was burning—usually just before he became numb.

'Yes,' the bishop continues, 'She said the well was a magical world filled with treasure hidden there by pirates. Some thought she had gone crazy. Personally, I think she heard of the stories from Orino Island. Have you heard those?' He doesn't wait for an answer. 'The tales of the rich merchants putting their gold down the wells to keep it safe when the island was invaded. It would be natural, stuck down a dark hole like that, for a child to let her imagination run wild at such a time, I think.'

Savvas can see her wide eyes staring up from the bottom of the well, the blue circle of sky above her. Maybe she shouted? No maybe about it. She was sure to have shouted. How long did she scream unheard? Now she says so little, as if she no longer wants the world to hear her. She gave the world its chance and it was not there for her. Poor thing. He will not be like the rest of the world. He will take his time to listen to her.

'Well, I'm glad you are settling in.' The bishops speaks briskly, as if wanting to round off the conversation, his duty done. Savvas tries to recall the things he wanted to bring up, areas that did not satisfy him with his situation, but nothing will come to mind, just Nefeli's pale browny-green eyes peering at him out of the darkness of his mind.

The phone purrs. The bishop has gone. He feels himself to have been totally ineffectual. He must pull himself together. Perhaps it is better to put what he has to say to the bishop in writing. One thing is for sure: he must continue with his demand for a car. It is time to organise his thoughts, start a list. Returning his phone to his bag, he falters, caught by a little wave of excitement as he spots the blue book he found in the tree's roots.

At the bureau, he compares the writing in the front of the poetry book with that in the diary. It is the same.

It may be a personal diary but the man is dead; there is no one to mind. Besides, anybody in his position would do the same. He flips open the first page and sits down to read. It opens with a few reflections, a few thoughts about life in general, the odd note to remind himself of mundane things such as funerals and baptisms he had to perform. The writing gives a sense of despondency. The tone lifts at one point in a long passage about a tree that fell in a storm and crushed the village shop. It seems that this event caused Sotos' beliefs in mankind to rise that day, as the whole village worked together to help the people trapped inside and to rescue the goods from the rain. But a few entries later, the despondency returns.

The handwriting becomes less clear as the diary passes through time, more scrawled, as if his pen increasingly scratched into the paper. A few pages further, and some of it stops making sense. Words repeated and spiritual things are referred to in very abstract ways. The thoughts of a rambling old man.

By an ink blot, in capitals, are the words GOD FORGIVE ME. Savvas turns back a few pages to find out what this refers to, and the writing here is intelligible, clear. He is drawn in.

'I should not go.' Savvas creates Sotos' voice in his head. He makes it old and shaky, a bit gravelly but kind, soft. The voice of a man who would give his house away.

'I should not have remained there yesterday. But I did not walk away, I stayed, unable to move. When it was over, I all but ran indoors.

Shame must have been emblazoned on my face, my sin visible to the world. But to go again today, I cannot excuse as an accident. It will be a deliberate choice and a very definite sin, not just against God's word but also against Nefeli herself. But the air in this big empty house is suffocating so even if I do not go there I must be outside.'

The journal must span the time Sotos moved from the big house to the small house. Savvas releases any guilt that remains for reading the diary. There could be something in here that is useful. Useful for the church to re-acquire the grand house. He reads on with enthusiasm.

'I could not overcome my urges. Once outside, other than the place I must not go, I could find nowhere to sit to write. So I thought to return my journal to its hiding place. The sun's heat was intense even under the olive trees, so the walk to replace my book could not be a quick one. My limbs felt like I was walking through warm honey, so lazy are my reactions at this time of year, when it is so hot. After returning my diary to its safe place, I stood and stretched. I must straighten out these days after I bend down. My old limbs are stiffening by the day. But in stretching them out, I did the very thing I promised not to do. Once my eyes had landed on the open window in the cottage I could not look away. Within a minute, she was there. I stepped back behind the tree and, God forgive me, I watched again!

'She followed the same routine. The shower turned on, she slowly disrobed, brushed her hair, wound it in a knot on top of her head, and stepped under the cascading water. Her movements so lithe, so graceful. She has no idea of her beauty. It is rare to see the hair off her face, but a more stunning countenance is impossible to imagine. The scar on her forehead was not invisible from the distance I was at, but it was not a desire for a clearer view of that which drew me closer. Running like an animal from behind one tree to the next, creeping up on her like a thief, I wanted to see the water run over her skin, every detail of her femininity. I was so close that if I had whispered her name, she might have heard me but for the sound of the water. The wet made her skin shine. Her eyes with those dark lashes closed against the stream of the shower. She sighed as the water cooled her and my hand went under my cassock. I am not sure how long I was like that.

'That was when it happened.

'From around the side of the big house, around the well, Maria came seeking me out.

'She saw. She saw everything and with one look, she condemned me as strongly as I condemned myself.

'My hand dropped from its hidden place but I could go nowhere. For all the world, I did not want to go towards Maria, to hear the words that accompanied that look. Besides, if I moved, Nefeli would have seen me, so I remained like a rabbit in torchlight. Fixed, not looking at Nefeli but at Maria instead, who, after her denouncing stare, turned on her heel and marched away. I remained hiding behind that tree, now forcing myself to look at the ground until the sound of running water stopped and I felt sure Nefeli had towelled, dressed, and left the small room.

'I ran to the back door of the house but instead of going up to my rooms, I went down into the cellar, where I slithered down the wall and sat on the floor, muttering out loud, pretending my words were prayers. But in my heart, I was damning God for giving me desires and then denying me a way to satiate them. Why would he put such a woman in my path? His ways are not mysterious; they simply make no sense. How can I believe in a God with such little compassion? A God that gives us dementia and strokes and cancer and women like Nefeli?'

Savvas looks up from his reading. This is the same God who said he could marry before he was ordained but not after! The same God who killed both his mama and his baba before they reached any great age. The God who drove his mama to make him lie in the shape of a crucifix on the church floor for hour after hour whilst she arranged the flowers to make the place pretty for the following Sunday. He can understand Sotos' disquiet. Especially about putting Nefeli in his path. In both their paths.

He turns a few pages. It seems something new has occurred.

'I cannot control myself when he comes calling on her. The rage in me starts in the pit of my stomach, and I feel sick. But then the feeling tightens like a knot and with it comes energy and the energy turns into power that courses down my limbs, making my hands ball into fists, giving me the energy of my youth. At first, I was concerned for her safety, that he should not harm her or hurt her emotionally or otherwise. Has his mama not confided in me countless times, telling me of her son's extreme emotions, telling me of her fears for her safety when he drinks to excess? But my own rages against him did not last long. Soon I found myself daydreaming about accidents he could have. Nothing fatal, just the sort of thing that would make him less desirable: a twisted leg, a scarred face. Then these became fantasies about accidents in which I was the assaulter, my fist in his eye, my foot crashing down on his nose. Such shameful thoughts, but where is God when I need Him? Is He here to give me strength, or is He giving children bone cancer and having rats nibble the toes of the old who cannot move their limbs?'

The rest of the page is blank. Savvas turns it over and the writing continues.

'I have not written for a few days. I have been studying my bible and focusing on prayer. But for what? For God to put them sitting on the well's edge, discussing their future. The shutters and window were open; it was not as if I was eavesdropping. No—God wanted me to hear. Nefeli's voice almost so soft I could not make out her words, but his were loud and strong.

'"With the income from my land and the olives here at the back of your house, if your mama will give them over to you, we can afford to live. The papas can marry us!"

'How triumphant he sounded. How knowledgeable he seemed about the value of the olives. Well, I had news for him: this papas was not going to marry them. I remained rigid, listening to every word. My neck was so tense, I was so strung out I thought I might snap a ligament if I turned my head away. In the end, I didn't move from that room all that day, even after Nefeli and her suitor had left the rendezvous. The sun went down, the lights in the village came on. The dogs started their evening chorus, the bells of sheep and goats as they were taken in for the night accompanying them. Shutters began to be closed with that familiar wooden bang in the homes all around the church, and I continued to sit. I sat until I decided on this plan.

'If it is the olives that will allow her to marry, I will take the olives away. I know that this is an evil decision but the jealousy that rages within me knows no rest. I want to strike out at him, at my impotency in life, at God. The olives come with their house, so I will take their house away. But I cannot leave them homeless. I do not wish to cause Nefeli herself suffering. I just wish to show her that this man, this suitor, has no real regard for her. But even as I write these words, an idea has come to me. There is only one of me, and I need very little space. In fact, I would prefer not to rattle around in this big house, where the echoing walls do nothing but remind me of my loneliness. The empty rooms mock my status. The barren kitchen and single bed jeer at my solitude. The air hangs heavy and still and undisturbed and within these walls, I am locked inside my own head, a witness to life through these eyes sockets but unable to partake. I am caged in my seclusion. So I will give over the big house to Nefeli and her mama! They can clatter about this big house and it will give Nefeli nothing that would attract a local farming boy. It is just a pile of stones that needs a lot of maintenance. A soulless building that is hard to keep warm in winter and cool in summer. It is a burden. It will ensure that she never marries, as I will make it that it is hers after her mama dies. But—and as I think these thoughts, I cannot justify these actions other than delighting in the feel the power of evil that is really digging deeply into me—she will not own the house. I think I do not have the power to give it to her, so she will never be in a position to either sell it or rent it out. Ha, no! She can just have use of it, be responsible for its upkeep. A non-transferable burden that she must maintain. Like the burden she is to me, the weight she creates in my heart. If I cannot have her, then no-one can.

'Reading back, I can hear how hard my words sound. If I thought there was any other way, I would take it. Although I even doubt this. Such little pleasure is offered me as a priest but I am finding pleasure in my plans to twist her life. Besides, I have sat here and mulled this over hour after hour, but what other course of action do I have? I really believe I would denounce the church if she would have me, but I am old and she is young. She would never consider me as a husband. Besides, I have no trade at which to make a living. And I suspect, no—I know—it is not her wifely qualities that I am seeking. That is not where my head goes to when I think of her. I think many things, but cooking and keeping house are not in those dreams. Where I want to go is far from a union sanctified by God and if I cannot go there, I will not let anyone else to go there in my stead. If God has made this world so unjust, then I will be unjust too. I am after all made in His likeness, am I not?'

Another blank page, then a leaf of abstract drawings, shapes, scrawls. The pen digging in so deeply that there is a hole through the paper in one place.

Savvas cannot help himself. He feels driven to read on.

'It has been a while since I have put pen to paper here. The days have been filled in conversations with Babis. He knows the law better than I expected for one so young. Together, we have made out papers for Nefeli and her mama to take the house. Each evening, I go to the tree and I watch her at the same time in her ablutions. I feel no shame anymore. I feel nothing.

'Maria came around, insinuating and fussing. So I told her good things happen to people who think only good and that bad things happen to people whose minds focus on the wrongdoings of others. She almost accused me of talking rubbish. So a day later, I took her bicycle from her front yard. I had no idea why I was taking it or what I intended to do with it but as I walked past it in the black of night, it felt like justified revenge. I have hidden it in an unused mud brick barn in an olive grove down towards the sea. It has given me some satisfaction, as she has done nothing but talk about her stolen bike ever since. She believes the children of the village are against her, that there is a vendetta. When she mentioned her missing bicycle to me, I reminded her of our conversation about bad coming her way for seeing bad in others, and she went very quiet. If she thinks it is God punishing her, perhaps she will stop. And if she suspects it is me, she will be scared of what more I am capable. I too wonder this.

'What I do know is that I no longer care what Maria thinks just as long as she leaves me alone with her accusing looks and belittling sneers.

'Today, I spent the afternoon with Nefeli and her mama. Nefeli filled my senses and I found it difficult to concentrate. Her hair is becoming more golden with each sun-filled day that passes, her skin has turned honey brown, and I swear her eyes have lightened. I notice the little bit of weight she carried around her hips over the winter has gone and I can imagine that some would say she is almost too slender. But I see her as a cat, lithe and supple.

'When Babis finally made it clear what I was offering, Nefeli's mama accepted it on both their behalf, but without much enthusiasm. As Babis pressed the point of what an extraordinary gift this was, I could see that the old woman at least made an effort to pretend it was a gracious gift, but it was clear that neither of them really wanted to be uprooted from their home and forced to live within these vast walls. But I don't care any longer. The deed is done and tomorrow we will exchange living quarters.

'The other advantage is that she will no longer shower in a room that is visible from the outside of the house, so at least I am also saved that temptation/torture.'

Savvas raises his eyes from the diary and rubs them before crossing himself three times, muttering some praises to God. It is so easy to understand what Sotos was going through, and yet also clear that he was going mad. Does that make him, Savvas, a truly compassionate person, being able to see so clearly someone else's point of view, or does it denote that he, too, is capable of going mad? He rubs the sweat off his forehead with the palm of his hand and bites on the inside of his lower lip.

'All day, we went backwards and forwards with Nefeli and her mama's things. For me, I took little from the big house to the cottage, but it was a chance to clear things out and I burnt many items in the olive grove. I also gave much away to the children in the square to take home to their own mamas. Later, walking into the corner shop around lunchtime, I heard the end of a conversation between Marina the shop owner and her daughter-in-law Irini, saying that I was such a good man to be giving so much away to the people of the village. I felt such a fraud. I almost turned away but Marina had seen me through the window. They both wished me a hearty "good day", but I found it hard to meet their gaze. They would take no money for the bread and cheese I wanted. I was insistent but to no avail and as I left, I heard the one say to the other what a modest man I was. If only they knew.'

Following this passage are several pages of dark ink drawings and illegible writing, then suddenly clearer, in a bold hand.

'When I found her, I could not help her in any way. I called the ambulance and the village doctor but other than that, I just sat with her. One side of her face was contorted; she sounded drunk. Later, I heard it was a massive stroke and that she would need round-the-clock care until she recovered. Nefeli seems to have been in shock ever since. There has been no one to do my washing or make my meals, so I have been living on bread and cheese and I have not changed my *anteri* for two weeks. It is grey with dust.

'There has been no sign of Nefeli's young man since her move to the big house and her mama's stroke. I am pleased about this. But Nefeli has taken to hanging the wet washing out on the front balcony. The sheets cling to her form, wrap around her curves. I know the times she does the washing and I wait hidden behind a half-closed shutter to watch her hanging out the clean, wet linen. I try to busy myself at these times to spare myself this ordeal, but things conspire so I am always by that half-closed shutter when she is about this work.'

Savvas wants to burn the book, destroy it completely. It is sucking him into a place he does not want to go. All the thoughts he has managed to push into some dark recess of his mind are being drawn forward and he finds himself not only understanding Sotos' words but agreeing with them. But even though he knows that discarding the book will do more good than reading on, he is compelled to continue.

'I am now being punished for all my wrong doings!' the next page begins.

'Nefeli's mama looks like she is not going to recover from this second stroke. The doctor has concluded that her condition is stable. Nefeli must assume her role as carer is a permanent one and I have had correspondence from the church telling me that if Nefeli's mama cannot continue her duties towards the church, then they cannot be paid by the church. This is a blow that can only be reconciled in one way. Nefeli must take over her mama's duties. So now I am to be tortured by her making my meals and cleaning my cottage. The alternative is that Nefeli and her mama will starve. You see how I am tested. If I was a truly evil man, I would let them starve. I do not need Nefeli to come into my home, especially now my home is so small and her every movement will be within arm's reach for me.

'I have taken to reading poetry to find some peace in my soul. It does me more good than praying these days, but sometimes the poems are too close to the truth, the torture I now suffer daily as Nefeli makes herself my housekeeper. I have begun to think she has bewitched me on purpose, that the evil is hers.

'It has been a month since I last wrote in this journal—or prayed, for that matter. My torture continues, my thoughts grow blacker and blacker. I swear Nefeli knows exactly what she is doing.

'I am afraid. Not of anything outside of myself but of what is within.

'Do not let me harm her. Or her me!'

Savvas turns the pages quickly, his heartbeat sounding in his ear. But there is no more. The pages are blank, white and pure. Sitting back, he exhales.

'How did he die?' The words come almost unbidden, but there is a growing disquiet and he looks around the room. Was he found dead in here, on the bed? He looks through the door to the chair by the fireplace. Was he found dead there? He shivers and feels for his crucifix through his robes. Wherever he died, he took his secret with him. The village thought of him as a saint as he gave away his possessions and moved into the smaller house. He himself has heard nothing but praise from every quarter. But after seeing his state of mind through his writing, Savvas cannot believe his predecessor died a natural and calm death.

But the good news, from reading through these pages, is that it seems Nefeli's mama at least was not in favour of the move from the cottage to the big house, so maybe the move back again will be met with pleasure? Now, however, he must write letters to the bishop. He needs a car and he is sure there are other things if he concentrates his mind.

Two weeks later, a four-wheel drive Mercedes is delivered to the church, much to the intense interest of the villagers, and in particular the tanned boys who play football in the square. The sun reflects off its black surface as the high-seated vehicle rolls through the square, turns up by the corner shop, and pulls to a halt on the paved area outside the church. The boys are the first to press their noses against the windows, greasy fingers smearing the paintwork. An old man leaving the kafeneio in the main square hobbles up to join them.

'Papas, how fast can it go?' a young boy asks.

'Papas, is it bulletproof like the Catholic Pope's?' a teenager asks with a slight teasing edge to his voice. It seems they teach the young all religions these days.

'Solid cars,' the old man announces. 'Bought my son one for his taxi job. Runs even when it is raining.'

Savvas looks at him twice, but the man seems serious.

A second man arrives, folds his arms, looks at the big shiny beast with a glint in his eye. He unfolds his arms and puts them in his front pockets to lean over and look at something a little closer inside the wheel arch.

'Hmm,' he grunts. Savvas waits for what is about to follow but the man says no more, just continues to stare before pulling a card from his pocket.

'You'll be needing this,' he says finally to Savvas and hands him the card before walking away. The card reads, *'Alekos garage. Tractors, cars, mopeds.'* Savvas looks into the wheel arch to see if he can see what Aleko could see, but there is just a thin layer of dust on the new, shiny paint.

A couple of people use the car as an excuse to loiter and chat, causing others that are passing also to stop and join in the conversation. Savvas recognises most of them from his Sunday morning service. He recognises more of the women perhaps than the men. The men have work as their excuses on Sundays; trees that won't wait to be tended, tractors that need to be tinkered with, animals that must be fed. But even though the male population has, in part, been absent, Savvas feels that over the last couple of weeks, he has made his status known and the majority of them are showing him suitable reverence.

There are one or two of the older ladies who think they have seen it all before and have offered him advice with very little respect, but he has dismissed these, firmly putting them in their places. The one he keeps his eye on, though, is Maria. There is nothing in the way she acts towards him that denotes what she witnessed of his predecessor. Sotos' secret seems to be safe with her. How many other secrets does she have? Come to that, how many secrets does everyone else in the village have? He looks about at the faces. They might all know things, about Sotos, about him, about the church.

It is a bad time for Maria to come across from her house. She looks over the car with disdain, shielding her eyes from the sun's glare with her hand. Above the bonnet, the air rises in shimmering waves.

'A very pretty toy,' she begins. With her presence, the boys return to their game of football and the others who had been using the car as an excuse to take a break and chat melt away. It seems he is not the only person who tries to avoid Maria's company.

'It is easy,' Maria says, folding her own arms and standing beside him, 'to fall into the ways of mankind.'

'It is a car, Kyria Maria. I need it for church business.' He would like to take it for a drive now, smell the leather interior. Take it for a spin into Saros perhaps, park on the sea front and sit having coffee overlooking the bay.

'An earthly desire,' Maria mutters through gritted teeth.

'Kyria Maria, I appreciate your sentiment, but please rest assured you have no need to concern yourself about my spiritual life.'

Maria looks up to the grand house where Nefeli is throwing a sheet over the stone balustrade of the balcony to air. Savvas is grateful that in this moment, the sheet is not wet and clinging to her. The sight of her attending to her domestic duties, even though it is a commonplace, trivial thing, makes the heat in his cheeks rise.

'I have seen how quickly a man can fall,' Maria says and her gaze, which is now on him, seems to see right into every thought he has ever had. Her penetrating look creates flashing images in his head of his mama spreading him in a crucifix position on the cold floor as a punishment. He forces himself into composure.

'Maria, please do not play games with me. If you have something to say, then say it.' His guilt twists into anger.

'What did they tell you about your predecessor?' Her voice is low so it does not carry, but Savvas looks around the square anyway.

'He was a good man,' he retorts, as if this is the end of the conversation. But his words do not sound convincing.

'Men are good till they fall. I suppose they told you he died of a heart attack?'

It would be wisest to stop this conversation right now, but his curiosity is too strong. She 'tuts' and lifts her chin, rolling her eyes, a Greek *'No!'* 'He did not die of a heart attack.'

Savvas' limbs tense rigid, waiting for her to say more. He cannot ask her, that would be tantamount to encouraging gossip, and it would admit that she has power, and knowledge that he wants it. It would most definitely imply his interest, which he feels very strongly that it is better to conceal. If he stares hard enough, the shiny new car will appear to be the focus of his attention.

'He died under the greatest sin of them all, in a bid to cover his other sins,' she finally says. Then there is a deliberate pause before, with a great deal of air, she expels a single word: 'Suicide.'

Savvas closes his eyes, bites his lower lip, and tries to maintain his calm exterior. On opening them again, he turns to face her.

'I think you have said enough.' The tightness in his voice matches a constriction in his throat.

'I found him. I thought he was sleeping. His cassock was pulled up above his knees and his legs were bright red. It was a scene no God-fearing woman should have to see. I was about to leave him to his slumbers but something made me stay. I pulled down his cassock and I shook his sleeve to rouse him, but his head rolled in a way that was not natural.'

'You've said enough, Kyria Maria.'

'Carbon monoxide poisoning. He had stuffed clothes up the chimney. My clothes, that he had taken from the washing line, and then he had burnt charcoal in a pan. And I will tell you something else. There was a bottle too, an empty bottle of Metaxa brandy. And sleeping pills. I took the empty packet so they weren't found, along with the bottle, and burnt my clothes.'

'Kyria Maria, I forbid you to say anything more.' She is colluding with him. She is telling him she performed a cover-up. Maria will not be silenced.

'It was her.' She glances towards the balcony. There is no Nefeli there now, but Savvas knows who she means.

'Kyria Maria, I do not know what you are trying to say and nor do I want to know. It is not your place to say these things or to judge.' The words fall one after the other but guilt is creeping all over him, consuming him. He has lusted after Nefeli too and Maria's confession, her admission of her cover-up, isn't that her way of pointing out his future path if he continues on the same route?

'She might not have actually lit the charcoal but if she didn't, she may as well have done it,' Maria whispers.

'Kyria Maria, I will hear no more!' And with these words, he strides away from her toward the church with such a pace, he can feel his cassock slap against his calves as he walks.

'Kick it back, Papas,' a boy shouts as his ball heads towards Savvas' feet, but he is in no mood for games. Going straight into the church, locking the door behind him, down the aisle he kneels and cries for his freedom, his loneliness, and his mama to be there.

The car drives well. It has such power, he can be in Saros in less than five minutes if needed. After his emotional moment in the church, he jumped behind the wheel and, once out of the village, his foot was heavy on the accelerator, topping a hundred kilometres an hour on the straight sections with no effort. The smell of the new leather lifted his senses, the plastic dashboard adding to the aroma. By the time he arrived in Saros, pulling up outside the first café he came to, he felt almost like his old self again. The coffee was good and his freshly baked croissant tingled the hairs in his nose. The second croissant satiated his hunger and the third, which was filled with chocolate, was a delightful indulgence. Sitting there, wiping crumbs from his thin beard, looking out across the sparkling blue sea where a small fishing boat putters out of the harbour, it occurs to him that he just isn't a country person. Now that he is in town, his soul feels soothed, his senses satiated. In the village, there is nothing to distract him: no shop windows, no cafés worth sitting in, no men in suits, women in their finery. His village work isn't life, it is just existence. He might think again about asking the bishop to reposition him.

With a certain reluctance, he drives slowly back to the village. He is somewhat revived by his brief sojourn in the town but the whitewashed cottages and neatly flowered gardens close in on him as he draws into the village. Looking up to the clear blue sky, he blocks out as much as he can of the rural scene, keeping one eye on the road ahead, and pulls up beside the church. Opening the door of his new car lets the new smell escape and the heat enter. The days are becoming hotter and hotter now. The cicadas have started their relentless mating call and he has ordered a catalogue of vestments. He needs to buy a cassock for the summer; otherwise, he will die from this heat. Unlocking the door to his little cottage, it occurs to him that he could even demand an air conditioning unit for the place. It is totally unreasonable not to have one. The thought of this concession to civilisation cheers him a little.

The catalogue has arrived and the postman, Costas, who does come to his services, has pushed it under the door. Perhaps he will get a silk cassock. They say silk is warm in the winter and cool in the summer.

With the door closed behind him, it is not unpleasant to be back in his cottage. To a degree, he has grown accustomed to the space. Although outside home, the village is very parochial, once he is inside his little house, everything seems less pressing. One thing the village has taught him so far is that there is no rush. Life continues. That attitude of the villagers seems to have got into his bones.

His phone rings.

'Savvas, did the car arrive safely?'

'*Kalimera*, Bishop. Yes, it is fine. Is it hot where you are?'

'Oh my, yes. The summer is upon us, I fear.'

'You have air conditioning, I take it?'

'Oh, yes indeed. Of course.'

'Then you are a lucky man, Bishop!'

'Ah, I see. You have not, I take it?'

Savvas does not answer this.

'Are you still there?' the bishop asks.

'Just mopping my brow, Bishop.'

'Very well, I will see what I can do, but expenses are not what we want right now, Savvas my friend.' The bishop clears his throat. 'This new government, I think they have it in for us! They want us, the church I mean, to pay our own way! Pay priests and bishops ourselves, from church funds. I think they forget how much the church did for this country when we were occupied by the Turks!'

Savvas takes the phone through to the bedroom and sits down at the bureau, where he can look out into the olive grove through the window. He did not shut the casement last night, nor the shutters, and the sounds of goat bells coming through the trees had soothed him to sleep and later, in the small hours of the morning when he woke from a dream in which Nefeli preached a sermon with Maria's voice, the gentle rustle of the olive leaves against each other caressed him back to his slumbers.

'If that comes to pass, then each church will need a big windfall from somewhere.' The bishop speaks with enthusiasm. 'They are also rumours that we may have to pay taxes. We must keep our wits about us. By the way, I do not recall how much you raised for the insulation of your church in America?'

A-ha! Now it becomes clear why the bishop has called. Maybe the church is more cunning than he thought and this is the reason he was brought over to Greece in the first place. This is his strength; he is good at raising money. With a long, drawn-out expiration of air, he feels like he has suddenly come home. He is in his comfort zone, as the world at large expresses these things.

But the bishop does not wait for a reply and Savvas feels very certain that the bishop knows exactly the amount, probably to the last cent.

'Although,' the old man continues, 'I have to say I am not personally bothered as I will retire soon, which of course leaves this bishopric open for a good man to come up.' There is no subtlety in what he is inferring. Savvas estimates a bishop's wage and envisages the colourful embroidered vestments on his own person. Within this brief dream also comes the big house as his home and Nefeli in her white apron, tending his domestic needs.

The bishop has chosen the right man. Savvas doubts that there is another priest in all of Greece who is as sharp as him when it comes to funding. The bishopric is his for the taking. All he needs to do is a little work here and there. His first task will be to acquire the grand house for the church. He jots down a note to himself to call Babis the village lawyer.

'I hear you, Bishop.'

'Good man, good man. And I will see what I can do about authorising a small air conditioning unit.'

Savvas mutters his response, suddenly distracted by a thought he is amazed he has not had before. Doesn't that man who was praying so earnestly in church last Sunday own an electrical shop in Saros? Perhaps he needs some spiritual guidance, someone to pray with him, ease his concerns. But he will not tell the bishop this until it is done. Getting this man to install air conditioning at no cost to the church will be the first of many little successes that he will have that he can draw to the bishop's attention, making him the obvious man to fill his shoes when he is ready to retire.

There are goats in his olive grove now. A tall, barrel-chested man is walking with a measured pace amongst them. The bells around the animals' necks ring out an idyllic cantata; the occasional warbled throaty aria accompanies. Savvas stabs his phone to bring up Babis' number and arranges a meeting. Babis might also know the name, and maybe other things, of the man who owns the electrical shop in Saros.

It has been a roller coaster of an emotional ride settling into the village, but if he can keep his mind where it is now, firmly set on the needs of the church, all that he deserves will follow.

There is a tap on the door, which startles him as he did not expect Babis so soon. The door pushes open before he can reply, so he knows it is Nefeli.

'Here is your cassock, Papas, all washed.'
She hangs it on the back of the door on a coat
hanger she has brought with her.

'Thank you.'

Then she goes straight to the sink and begins
washing up the pots from his breakfast. He is so
used to her being around now that her presence
no longer disturbs him. She actually calms him
with her quiet movements, her grace, and her
tidiness. Although she still does not speak a
great deal, she seems to have grown comfortable
with him, too. He certainly does not feel towards
her as Sotos felt. What he feels is far more gentle.

She takes the broom and starts to sweep.
Now that the heat is upon them, the dust seems
to grow out of the floorboards almost hourly.
Nefeli is very conscientious and not only sweeps
but mops his little cottage every day. The motes
spin and dance in the sunbeams, her white
apron blindingly clean in the light, her hair
glistening as it falls over her face.

He should broach the subject of her moving
into the cottage before Babis is here.

'Nefeli, how would you like to move back
home?' It comes out rather more direct then he
envisaged.

The sweeping stops. She looks at him, her
pale eyes accentuated by her wide pupils.

'I mean back here, into the cottage,' he clarifies.

'No.' She sweeps on.

'Why?'

'Because Mama she is used to where she is and it is hers for life.'

'And?' He softens his voice, sensing she has more to say.

'And if I moved back here, how can I be sure there is security for her life?'

'In the same way that you had when you used to live here.'

'The cottage came with the job. The church can take both away. It is not enough now she is as she is.' Another rise of motes in the sunlight as her broom takes action again.

'I could do the same with this cottage as my predecessor did with the big house. I could legally write it over to you.'

'She is familiar with the big house.' The broom is set to one side and the mop bucket is filled.

'Nefeli, I am not about to make you homeless. As long as I am here, you are assured of your position.' From under her hair, she looks at him to see if truth shows in his face. He knows it does.

'They might move you.' Her eyes are so wide now, she looks scared, fragile. He wants to put his arms around her, assure her not to fear. When she is in the room, he cannot imagine being anywhere else in the world. In fact, when she is in the room, nothing else seems to matter at all: not his work, nor the bishopric, nor the ownership of the big house.

'I will stay,' he announces, and the conviction he feels inside is a revelation to him.

She takes a step towards him, the mop bucket abandoned. His own heartbeat throbs at his temple. There is also a strange expansion in his chest which steals his breath and he recognises it as a yearning, a yearning to make her safe, take her in his arms and hold her gently, softly.

With long fingers, she strokes the hair from her face and looks him in the eye. The fear he usually sees there is subsiding. The scar on her forehead twists its ragged way into the hairline she has made visible. His hand reaches towards it, fingers pulsating to stroke the angry reminder but he pulls his arm back to his side.

'It was my home here, but with the move to the big house, I realised nothing is secure.'

'I will give it to you.' He cannot stop staring into her eyes. The rule that once ordained a priest cannot marry is a ridiculous one. In this moment, he would give up his calling to marry her. The church might be losing many good men for such a silly rule.

'You will give it to me?' A small frown flashes across her forehead but the scarred area does not move. A tractor rumbles somewhere outside in the village, but, right now, life outside of these walls has nothing to do with him. There is only Nefeli.

'Yes. I will give it to you.' The words create a smoothness to her countenance; her eyes are moist. Has he reduced her to tears? Does it mean that much to her? 'Babis is coming round; I will ask him to make up the papers. It will be yours.' Her eyes moisten all the more and a single tear rolls over and runs down her cheek. Again, his arm moves and his hands reaches, this time to stroke the tear away. He feels she would let him, maybe he should just do it. He lets his arm finish its upward arch and his thumb reaches her cheek. Slowly and gently, he wipes away the tear. Her whole body seems to relax and he would give anything to kiss her!

His weight rolls onto the balls of his feet, readying him to move, to cover the small distance between them.

A sharp rap on the door dispels the fixation, sending the room spinning into collision with reality.

'Papas? It's Babis.'

Nefeli's hair falls. She looks to the floor. Her limbs take on their usual tightness of movement and she takes mop and bucket to the fireside, where she resumes her work.

Lifting the latch, Babis pushes in with briefcase and papers in each hand, heavy steps and sweating profusely. He smells of aftershave and fried food.

'*Kalimera*,' he says in Nefeli's direction and dumps everything he is carrying on the table. 'And *Kalimera* to you too, Papas. I hope you are settling in alright. So, what can I do for you?'

'Coffee?' Savvas asks.

'Water,' Babis replies and before the word has left his mouth, Nefeli is taking glasses from the shelf.

'My God, Papas, have you no air conditioning in here? You will roast like an Easter goat come August!' Babis sits heavily into a chair, taking out a handkerchief to mop his forehead.

'It is being arranged,' Savvas says and looks to Nefeli to see if she is alright. The change of mood was so sudden, he feels he is reeling.

'So, how can I help?' Babis takes a fat fountain pen from his shirt pocket and a notebook from his briefcase and waits, poised.

'One minute.' Savvas goes through to the other room and takes the stamped official paper from under the diary and poetry book in the bureau. 'This is the old agreement, of Nefeli and her mama moving into the big house, but this cottage is her home, so I think it is best that we make the old agreement null and void and strike up a new agreement that gives her the rights to this cottage again.' He is not sure now if what he is doing is the right thing.

Would Nefeli want the old agreement if she knew that the big house would be for her life, too? Or would giving her the small cottage be the greater security? It might be an idea to discuss it with her but as the bishop said, it is not always in peoples' interests to know everything. It might make the whole issue too complex for her. No, he should make the decision. She said that moving to the big house made everything seem impermanent, insecure. Well, he can reverse that. If the cottage is in her name, there can be no greater security in this life than that.

'You mean you want me to write up a tenancy agreement?' Babis asks.

'No, I want to sign the deeds over to her.' He looks at Nefeli wringing out the mop and then pouring the water from the bucket down the sink. She flashes a look at him, a twitch of a smile around her lips. The smell of the dusty water gurgling down the sink briefly takes over from Babis' aftershave.

'Really?' Now Babis looks at her, from her hair down her graceful figure to her feet and back.

A week passes and the heat is building daily. His silk cassock arrives smelling of the plastic bag it came in, but it is cool and feels heavenly against his skin. Babis finishes the deed transfer and, without any slip or fuss, Nefeli signs her relinquishment of the grand house and is presented with the deeds to the cottage.

Savvas is packing up his few possessions. They agreed today they would move. His phone rings.

'So, today is the day. Well done, my boy!' The bishop is full of energy. 'This is a big feather in your cap. The archdeacon is very pleased.' He rattles on about church business as Savvas takes his phone outside and watches Nefeli on the balcony, folding sheets and putting them into a box. In the week that has passed, he has watched her confidence blossom. Her hair is tied back now and the scar has faded as the skin on her forehead has tanned. She walks with more lift to her chin and she no longer seems afraid of the grace that flows through her limbs. She moves, now, with confidence. The bishop drones on as Savvas continues to watch until she disappears inside and comes out the front door.

'Sorry, Bishop. I have to go.' Savvas switches off his phone and tucks it in the box waiting by the cottage door. Nefeli is bringing her first bag of things. Her long apron seems whiter than normal, and the ribbon tying back her hair is equally white. Like her forehead, her arms are a shade darker now summer is here. She smells of jasmine and fresh air with hints of freshly ground coffee.

'I have very little to move so once I take these across, I can help you,' he offers.

As she passes him in the doorway, her forearm rubs against him. She makes no apology but stops to look him in the face and nods and blinks her acceptance of his offer of help. Even though her hair is tied back, it is loose enough to frame her face and add drama to her black-rimmed eyes. The sun behind her blurs her edges as if she is changing into light.

Despite the heat, the day is spent pleasantly moving things back and forth. The man who owns the electrical shop in Saros turns up with a workman to put in an air conditioning unit. He seems a little perplexed by the house exchange but leaves his worker to finish the job. It doesn't seem to take the electrician long and after gathering his tools, he waves them a hearty farewell. Nefeli is passing through a door that Savvas has just stepped in through from the other direction. She touches his hand, letting her fingers linger as she thanks him for the air conditioning unit.

'It will make Mama so much more comfortable.' Their faces are too close. Savvas feels almost sure that they will kiss. Until, without warning, she continues on outside.

Shortly after that, a dog joins them as if it is a game, sniffing each box and bag, ears flapping as it trots beside them, following their paths, turning around then back. They laugh in unison at the dog's curiosity.

It is only after they are nearly finished that Savvas notices Maria standing, arms folded, in her front garden, watching them. But he doesn't care. He has not felt this happy since before his mama died. Nefeli smiles at him as she passes with the last of her things.

Savvas stands at the doorway of his old home, looking in at her kneeling between boxes, unpacking and arranging. The sun streams through the open shutters, the place full of new life. She looks up at him hovering by the door.

'Come in!' she says.

'It is not my home to come in unbidden anymore,' he replies, and his laughter that accompanies the words is caught in his throat. The sight of her there, like a child surrounded by boxed presents, brings a surging feeling within his chest and he has to breathe in, expand his chest to make room for it.

'Is it really mine, Papas? I mean, really mine to do as I like with?' Her innocence is so much of her charm.

'To do just as you like. Paint it pink if you want.'

'And the land?'

'Yes, and the land.' This creates a lump in his throat. This was the reason why her home was taken from her in the first place. No land meant no marriage. Perhaps now she will marry. The feeling in his chest shifts. If she is ready to marry, and she could consider marrying him, then he will renounce his calling. Tears fill his eyes. Giving up the church is both a terrifying and a liberating thought. If he still feels the same in a day or two, he will carefully, so very carefully, bring the subject up with her, see how she feels. His instincts say she has very fond feelings for him, but his knowledge in these matters is very unsure.

'I think I will have to ask you every day for a week before I believe you,' she says.

'Then ask,' Savvas replies.

'Will you help me with Mama now?'

They walk side by side into the grand house.

Every day she asks.

'Is it really mine? And the land, too?'

'Yes, it is really yours. The land too,' he replies and they both smile.

After the second day, she adds on another sentence.

'Is it really mine? The land too? And all the trees?'

'Yes, it is really yours. The land too and all the trees.'

The third day she asks, 'Is it really mine? The land? The trees? The well?' It has become a game and he loves to play it.

'Yes, Nefeli. It is really all yours. The house, the land, the trees, and the well.' He wants to add, 'And me, I am yours too, Nefeli.' But he closes his mouth and keeps his lips sealed—for now.

From his new large bedroom, the window looks down onto the olive grove and many a time he watches Nefeli walking through the trees, graceful in her movements, a hand stroking across the bark, pulling on a low-hung leaf. She is there at night too, her skin shining in the moonlight. Her hair shimmers, unreal, as she looks up at the stars. At these moments, it takes all his willpower not to join her until one night, he can hold himself back no longer and he takes his own stroll, meeting her as if by surprise.

'Oh, Nefeli. You are out late.'

'And you, Papas.'

'Can you not sleep?'

'It is so beautiful.' Her gaze is into the trees, the leaves shiny or dull depending on the twist of the branch. 'Can you not sleep?'

Her scar looks angry in the pale moonlight, ugly and defacing. She may not find a suitor even now that she has the olives; men can be so fickle. But he is there.

'I was reading the bible and pondering on a text.' He waits for her to ask which one but she doesn't. 'Ecclesiastes 4:9-11. Do you know it?' She tuts her 'no' and pulls at a long grass by one of the tree trunks. 'It says "Two are better than one, because they have a good return for their labour."'

A flash of the whites of her eyes. He emboldens himself to continue.

'If either of them falls down, one can help the other up. But pity anyone who falls and has no one to help them up.'

The look she gives him now is not a kind one. Maybe she has misunderstood him. He must finish the quote so she is not in ambiguity.

'Also, if two lie down together, they will keep warm. But how can one keep warm alone?'

She throws her grass away. This is his moment. This is the second he must make himself plain. No better time will be offered him than this.

'If I were not a priest, Nefeli,' he begins. Her face is lit by the moon.

'If you were not a priest, things would be very different,' Nefeli states, looking him in the eye. It makes his heart race. It is beating so hard, she must be able to see it through his cassock.

'If I was not a priest, I would find a way to make a living. I believe I am very capable.'

'As all men are,' she replies simply.

'Would our relationship be different if I were not a priest, Nefeli?' There, he has said it. There can be no mistaking what he is asking.

'Of course,' and with it comes a smile. A bat chirps its agreement. A black bullet. She ducks. The flying rodent catches a strand of her hair. Her hand goes to her head to make all smooth. The bat peeps its position some distance away and calm is restored. But the tender moment is gone. He has been clear but she has not. She has left him with hope but not an assurance. In what way would they be different? In the way he is hoping or in another way? The bat sweeps again and take the remainder of the intimate mood with it, along with Savvas' courage.

The next day, she does not ask if the land, and the trees, and the well, and the house are really hers. A pain grips his heart and a tightness takes his throat, drying his mouth when he sees her.

The day after that is Sunday. The service is an easy one but the villagers have become used to his reflections at the end and he feels obliged to offer some wisdom. But he has no idea what topic he wants to teach, so he is unprepared and finds himself preaching from the heart. Eve as Adam's mate seems to be the message, but he is making little sense. As he tries to recall his bible quotes to give his monologue validity, something comes from some distant corner of his memory and he begins the verse, reciting each word as it comes.

'Proverbs five: May your fountain be blessed, and may you rejoice in the wife of your youth. A loving doe, a graceful deer.' From his neck to his cheeks comes an intense heat. He stammers as he remembers the final line. The congregation is silent.

Wetting his lips with his tongue, he tries to remain calm. The heat in his cheeks is not subsiding, and the final line needs to be spoken to complete his quote. What on earth made him recall this verse of all verses? He opens his mouth and out the words come. 'May her breasts satisfy you always, may you ever be captivated by her love.' A few of the women in the congregation gasp and nudge their husbands awake. Maria, who is in her usual seat right at the back of the church, stands, hesitates and then, noticed only by him, walks out.

But he has no concern over Maria. What on earth must Nefeli be thinking? She is staring at him wide-eyed. After the shock of his words have subsided amongst the churchgoers and they stop twittering amongst themselves, their attention is back on him, but his eyes are on Nefeli.

The village follows his gaze in unison. Nefeli tenses her back, becomes rigid. Savvas would do anything to take the words back, to take the collective focus away from her. There are only a few who remain looking at their prayer books; Marina from the corner shop for one, and Mitsos, who runs the local eatery, for another. He is grateful that not all in the village are the same. He brings the service to a quick end with a prayer and a blessing and then they file out, leaving Nefeli sitting by herself near the front.

Like the coward he feels himself to be in that moment, Savvas leaves by the side door to avoid her. Her and everyone else in the village.

Back at the house, he could cry over his stupidity. He may as well have shouted his feelings for her from the bell tower. It will not be him who is frowned upon. It will be her. Lost for what to do, he goes into his grand bedroom and lays on his bed, willing sleep to take away his thoughts. The smell of goats drifts through his window, along with the slow footfall of the shepherd. No hurry; an ambling walk. As his eyelids grow heavy, it occurs to him how much easier a layperson's life is, and in this moment he would swap all his status with that goat herder and the simple life he leads.

Towards the end of the day, but an hour later than normal, he can hear Nefeli downstairs preparing his evening meal. Maybe he should go and say something to her. Smooth the way again, apologise.

With the intention of doing something, anything, he leaves his glass of ouzo and the game of backgammon that he has been playing against himself on the balcony for the last two hours to slip, on silent feet, down the wide stairs.

She is by the sink and he has not seen her looking this miserable since he first arrived in the village. Her face is drawn and, although it seems in his mind a bit of an overreaction, it looks as if she has been or perhaps still is crying.

'Nefeli,' he begins, but she gives no sign that she has heard. 'Nefeli, it was with the best of intentions. I hope I didn't… I mean, I know how the village…' But it is as if she cannot hear him. Her face remains unmoving, blocking him out. His breath comes in short pants, his hands turn outwards, reaching, imploring. His feelings for her press against his rib cage, bursting from his soul. He can hold himself in no longer.

'For God's sake Nefeli, I love you!'

She turns her head so slowly. The tears are streaming down her cheeks. Her arms hang heavily, no longer cutting the bread, her hands just resting on the table. A greater picture of misery he has never seen. Her lips quiver as if she is about to say something. He wills her to speak, to say something, anything.

She takes a deep breath.

'She is dead.'

Savvas rocks back on his heels.

'What?' But he has heard what she said.

'Mama, she is dead.'

'Oh Nefeli.' And without a thought for himself, he is beside her, his arms around her as she sobs into his silk cassock. She remains there, shaking and sobbing, until he slowly guides her to the sofa so she can sit and then makes her a coffee. There is no need to speak, and so they don't. He makes her a sandwich but after a bite, she pushes it away. Her shoulders drop forwards, her hair hangs over her face as it has always done, and her defence walls are up. He sits with her.

Then, as he is thinking that perhaps he should do something, say something, she lifts her chin, forces a smile and says, 'Is the house really mine?'

She is inviting him to play.

'Yes,' he says kindly.

'And the trees?'

'Yes.' He takes her hand.

'And the well.'

'And the well.'' He strokes her knuckles.'

'And the land?'

'Everything around you is yours, Nefeli.' As he says this, he looks deeply into her eyes to let her know he is included in that deal. She sighs and there is the smallest of smiles.

Unlike in America, the funeral is carried out immediately. With the weather so hot and no facility to cold store the body, it is the only way. The bishop turns up in recognition of the years of service Nefeli's mama gave to the church. Marina from the corner shop also attends with Mitsos and his small-framed wife, Stella. Stella hands him an envelope and before the service begins, he opens it to find a request for him to bless the hotel's grand opening. There will be food and drink and music. Life goes on.

Savvas has written his own letter, addressed to the bishop. He did not spend very long agonising over it, nor did he even bother to word it well. It is straight and to the point.

'Bishop,' it reads, 'I thank you for your encouragement but it is with regret that I resign my position. I will complete the engagements on the books but I will be taking no more on past the end of the month.' The hotel blessing is included in that list of duties as well now, but he does not mind that so much. There will be food and wine there. Maybe Nefeli will go. He hands his own letter to the bishop when no one is looking, and the bishop takes it with a small frown and pockets it unopened.

Nefeli. Poor Nefeli, alone now. She has no mama and those moments of him consoling her in the kitchen have led him to believe that his feelings are returned. She heard that he loved her and she fell into his arms to sob. What further confirmation does he need?

Six people follow the hearse from the church to the graveyard, and the coffin is interred.

Three of the party disperse after the burial, leaving the bishop and Nefeli to walk with him back to the church. The bishop has his open letter in his hand and does not look happy. He looks from Savvas to Nefeli and back, but Savvas refuses to feel any guilt. She makes him happy, gives him reason to live, kills his greed and all in all makes him a better person. Surely that must be the best reason in the world?

He will share the joyful news that he has resigned with her later. Her mama's funeral is not the time. When they get back to the church, the bishop makes his excuses and leaves without a word about the resignation letter. Nefeli declares she needs time alone.

In the evening, he sits on his balcony drinking more ouzo and watches the sun go down. Technically, he muses, it is not his balcony any more. His home will be down in the cottage with Nefeli. His home will be amongst the olive trees with her. If the olives are not enough for them to live on, he will take a job in the nearby town of Saros. If that becomes a necessity, he will have to get his own car. The black four-wheel drive will be for the next priest. His own car, now that's a nice thought.

Maria comes out of her front door, catches sight of him, and shakes her head forlornly. It makes him smile now. She will get such a surprise when he invites her to his wedding. He will invite her and the whole village! Maybe if this hotel is a nice place, he can have the reception there.

One ouzo becomes two and two become three and before he knows it, the night has passed and cockerels are crowing and the first rays of the sun are in his eyes. There is also a noise outside of metal against wood. Surely it is too early for anyone to be up. Rubbing his face to encourage wakefulness brings the world into focus, but what he really needs is water before he can take any interest in what the village is up to. In the kitchen, he drinks a litre of tap water straight down and takes another back up to the balcony. Nefeli won't be here for another few hours to make his coffee. Another unusual sound comes from outside, from the side of the house, in the space between his house and the cottage.

Putting his glass down carefully on the balustrade, he leans over to see what is going on.

At first, it makes no sense. There is a pickaxe and a pile of ropes. The pickaxe is half-lodged under the well cover, which has been prised to one side. What on earth is going on? Nefeli will be horrified. Is this the church's work? He must go and stop whoever it is.

As he is resolving to take action, Nefeli calmly comes out of her cottage.

He rubs his face with both his hands, his fingers rotating on his eyeballs, trying to gain better focus, make sense of what he is seeing. Nefeli rolls up her sleeves, loops one of the ropes around her waist, and tugs to check the other end is secure. Once she is satisfied, she lowers herself over the edge and into the well.

Savvas gasps. He watches her disappear beneath the well's edge, hand over hand until there is nothing left to see. He thinks to go down, find out what is going on, but another part of him is in shock. He thought he knew her, that she shared her life with him, that he knew her thoughts, but this is something she has not even given him a hint about. This is something completely independent of him and it makes no sense. He would never revisit that church where he laid prone all those hours. He would nail the doors shut, bomb the place, have it levelled but he would not go inside, not for all the money in the world.

At first, his next thought seems a surreal notion. But then why else would she lower herself down there? It is crazy, but it is the only thing that makes sense. She simply wants to assure herself of the realities of what she experienced. See for herself that she created dreams to safeguard her sanity. It is easier for him; he never truly believed that he was lying on a beach or in front of a fire, but he could imagine touching the church floor to see if it is really as cold as he remembers it. Maybe that is what she is doing: proving that it is not that scary now she is grown and it is hers to do as she likes with. This is a new side he is seeing of her. A brave, bold, courageous side and he feels a tremendous sense of pride. What a women!

The rope, which had slackened, becomes taut again, and soon she reappears, hand over hand. He would never have given her credit for such strength. Her apron pocket is bundling and jolting against her skirts before her. Once on firm ground, she kneels, loosens her apron, and there are flashes and flames. The sun hits at angles, sending shards of light in all directions. The glints and blazes, glitterings and prisms of sunlight blind him so he cannot tell what he is seeing and only when the objects stop falling from her skirt to lay motionless on the ground is it clear what is there before her. In a heap lays a pile of gold coins, silver spoons, a small silver box, and a few other items that are indistinguishable from this distance.

Unable to move, he watches her fill a waiting bag with her trove, which she then carries into her cottage and closes the door behind her.

Savvas shuts his mouth, which has fallen open.

Maybe she kept this from him because she was not sure if it was a dream? Maybe she even wanted to surprise him. One thing is for sure: he will not have to get a job in Saros! The gold and silver hoard will be worth thousands! More than the value of the house. Should he wait for her to come to him or should he go to her now?

He should go to her. He has not even told her about the letter to the bishop yet! He will go down and tell her that he has quit the church and that they can now be married and she can show him the treasure!

He trots down the wide staircase, holding his cassock up between finger and thumb. His heart beats so hard, his chest feels like it might crack. The back door swings open as he runs into the olive grove, round the side of the house, and past the well. He stops just beyond the gaping black hole, and retraces his steps to stare down into the depths but doesn't linger and instead hurries on to tap lightly but rapidly on her door.

'Nefeli?' he calls.

After a few minutes, she opens the door a crack.

'Nefeli, it is me.'

She opens it wider, allowing him admittance. The gold is on the table. Some of the coins are stacked in towers, as if she has been counting them. The sight of it take his voice away and he just stares. There must be more wealth there than a person needs in a whole lifetime, no matter how well they live! After the initial distraction, he turns to her.

'Nefeli.' He wants to do this properly. He tries to slow his racing heart down, take it slowly. 'I once asked you if I was not in the priesthood, would you and I be different, and you replied yes.' He gazes into her eyes, trying to gauge her reaction. She is wide-eyed but does not offer any resistance to his words, and he allows himself to be encouraged. He lifts his cassock and drops to one knee.

114

'Nefeli, I have left the priesthood. Will you marry me?'

A frown, a smile, a chuckle, a straight face. She seems to go through a whole range of emotions. It takes some time for her to compose herself.

'Papas,' she begins.

'Savvas.'

'Savvas, it would take someone with a personal conviction strong enough to make that person become a man of the church for me consider them as a possible partner.' It is possibly the longest sentence he has ever heard her say. She looks down at him where he remains kneeling, her beautiful eyes, with deep, wide pupils reaching deep into his being.

'And I am that man.'

'Yes.'

'But now I am free.'

'You are.' She is smiling now.

'I am. I was a priest, and now I am not.' His excitement is making him tremble. It is difficult to keep his balance.

'So I could never marry you.'

Does she misunderstand?

'No you could not, but now you can. I am free of the priesthood.'

'And now you are free of the priesthood, I could never marry you.'

'No, you can.' This is not making sense.

'No, I cannot. I will not. If you are fickle with the calling of God, how much more fickle will you be with people?'

'But I love you.'

'You love yourself.' She does nothing to soften her words. There is a beeping outside. She goes through to the bedroom and returns with a stout leather bag. She sweeps her treasure into the bag and, snapping it shut, walks to the door.

'Goodbye,' she says.

'Where are you going?' Savvas doesn't care that he is losing all dignity, running after her as she marches to the waiting taxi. 'Nefeli, where are you going?'

She climbs into the backseat.

'Athens,' she inform the driver, who looks back at her with a frown. She fishes in her pocket and brings out some notes. The driver pockets them, smiling now.

'Nefeli? Nefeli? Are you coming back?'

She tuts and rolls her eyes; a very Greek 'no.'

And the square in front of the church is suddenly empty. There is just him, and Maria outside her front door, arms folded across her chest and a sneer playing about her mouth.

The bishop's car pulls up.

'Well here we are.' He leads the young man in the cassock from the chauffeur-driven car towards the grand house. 'This is your house and you have a help who lives there.' The bishop points to the cottage. Savvas ducks below the window ledge from where he has been watching. 'He is called Savvas. He used to be a priest but has lost his way a bit, so out of kindness, we let him live there and be caretaker, but let us know if he is not up to the job.'

'Oh, it is sad to hear when someone loses their way.' The young priest cannot be much more than twenty. His beard is hardly there at all.

'I think at one point, he became almost delusional.'

'Oh dear, nothing too awful, I hope.'

The bishop takes on his confidential tone.

'Well, between you and me…' He moves closer to the new priest but even his whispers carry through the cottage's open window. 'He said the girl that lived in the cottage before him killed her own mama! He said he found items of clothing that she had stolen from her neighbour stuffed up her chimney. He said that she had burnt charcoal in a pan in the sealed room.

Carbon monoxide poisoning. The girl herself has disappeared to Athens, and we cannot trace her, but then, why would we? The mind does funny things under stress.'

The bishop sighs before continuing. 'And if that were not enough, he claimed that this same girl killed the priest before him, too! It is hard to find sympathy for a man who goes to these lengths in his lies. But then, perhaps they are not exactly lies, if he believes what he says. His mind was focused on the material things in life, you see. One of his fantasies is that this same girl lowered herself down that well and came up with her skirts full of gold. We have tried to keep his state of mind out of public knowledge. It is not always a good thing for the people to know everything. No, indeed it is not! What this village needs now is a steady man like you. A steady man who can work towards both the good of God and the church.'

The young man is smiling and nodding with enthusiasm. But he stops suddenly and Savvas shifts his own position to remain hidden behind one of the shutters, following this new priest with his gaze.

Outside her door, opposite, with arms folded, stands Maria, appraising the new priest.